Nanny's nightmare

Emma reeled at the horrible coincidence that had sent her to the house where Diane, the woman Emma's father had wanted to marry—the woman Emma had driven away—had lived.

There was now no chance of ever being more to Kane than a very temporary neighbor. She'd ruined any such hope seven years ago, when she'd been sixteen, grief-stricken and outraged—and determined and devious.

She wondered whether she should tell Kane, but dismissed the idea. No, it was over and done with, long gone, and it didn't sound as though Diane came home from the other side of the world very often. Let sleeping dogs lie, Emma thought.

Dear Reader,

A perfect nanny can be tough to find, but once you've found her you'll love and treasure her forever. She's someone who'll not only look after the kids but could also be that loving mom they never knew. Or sometimes she's a he and is the daddy they are wishing for.

Here at Harlequin Presents® we've put together a compelling new series, NANNY WANTED!, in which some of our most popular authors create nannies whose talents extend way beyond taking care of the children! Each story will excite and delight you and make you wonder how any family could be complete without a nineties nanny.

Remember—Nanny knows best when it comes to falling in love!

The Editors

Look out next month for:

Accidental Nanny by Lindsay Armstrong (#1986)

ROBYN DONALD

The Nanny Affair

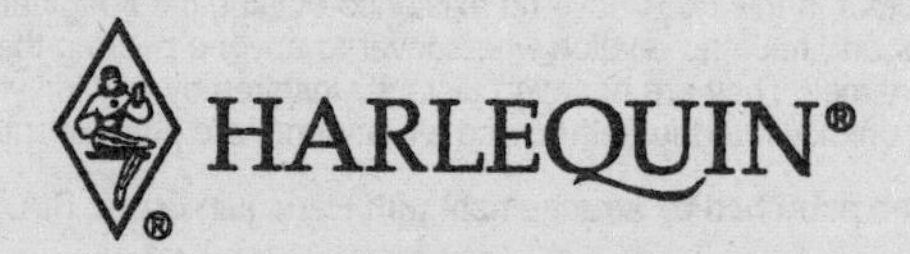

TORONTO • NEW YORK • LONDON
AMSTERDAM • PARIS • SYDNEY • HAMBURG
STOCKHOLM • ATHENS • TOKYO • MILAN • MADRID
PRAGUE • WARSAW • BUDAPEST • AUCKLAND

To Don and Lucky, and in memory of Morag

ISBN 0-373-11980-1

THE NANNY AFFAIR

First North American Publication 1998.

This edition published by arrangement with Harlequin Books S.A.

Printed in U.S.A.

CHAPTER ONE

'LUCKY! *No!*'

Emma Saunders deepened her normally gentle voice into an authoritative roar, but the barely half-grown dog ignored her, slithering beneath the bottom wire of the fence like an eel before racing towards the flock of sheep some two hundred metres away.

Their heads came up; a few of the nearer ones began to run, and Lucky recognised a new and exciting variation of chase. Barking, he set off after them.

Panic grabbed Emma beneath the breastbone. 'Lucky, *no*,' she yelled ferociously, not pleased when the elderly corgi at her side barked imperatively.

However, that summons did the trick. Reluctantly Lucky skidded to a halt, wistfully panting after the sheep, which were now in full flight across the paddock.

'Here!' Emma ordered, muttering, 'Thank you, Babe,' to the corgi as relief surged through her and her pulse rate slowed.

Realising he'd committed some unknown sin, Lucky approached carefully and with ingratiating whines. Her senses honed by adrenalin, Emma tried to ignore the car that drew up behind her.

It didn't work. The skin on her back prickled in a primitive warning. Because she didn't dare take her eyes off the puppy, every sound the driver made as he or she got out assumed vast significance. The solid thunk of the closing door almost made her jump.

A cold, dark, very male voice stated, 'If I see that dog chasing my sheep again I'll shoot him.'

Emma had to swallow to ease her dry throat. 'It won't

happen again,' she said without turning her head. Her voice sounded oddly tinny in her ears.

Although not yet a year old, Lucky's mostly Rottweiler blood—and dominant male genes—told him that Emma might need protection. In a streak of black and tan he hurtled beneath the fence and positioned himself on four stiff legs between Emma and the unknown man, hackles raised, ears slightly flattened as he watched with wary alertness.

'Heel!' Emma said sharply as she turned to face both man and dog.

Lucky stood firm. Not now! Emma thought, repeating the command. This was a tussle of wills she couldn't afford to lose. Her demand for obedience was not aided by the old corgi, who was eyeing the intruder with grave reserve.

'Heel!' Emma said steadily, refusing to accept the pup's offer of a compromise, which was to sit just in front of her, black and brown face turned implacably towards the strange man.

Emma hadn't yet looked directly at him, but from the corner of her eyes she could see that he took up too much room.

At least he understood dogs. Silently, with ominous stillness, he waited as she ordered again, 'Heel.'

Lucky didn't want to move, but he knew who was the leader in his particular pack. Unwillingly, keeping a cautious gaze on the stranger, he got to his feet.

Emma waited until he stood at heel before saying, 'Good boy. Sit.'

He sat.

After patting him, Emma lifted her head. Because the setting sun shimmered in a dazzling aura around the stranger's head she couldn't discern his features, but the rest of him was formidable enough to make her check an instinctive step backwards. She didn't need to see his face to be aware of an overwhelming presence, made more impressive by a curbed patience that sent a swift, chilling shiver through her.

Talk about dominant males! she thought, stubbornly refusing to be impressed. He and Lucky were a good pair.

Big—too big—the stranger had shoulders that would have done a rugby forward credit. They surmounted a magnificent chest that tapered to narrow, masculine hips above long legs. Neither trousers nor checked shirt hid the powerful muscles of a man who used every single one every day.

He loomed at least a foot above her five feet three inches, and every inch of that height was significant.

But it wasn't his physical configuration alone that fired Emma's senses. It was his stance—the lithe, disciplined authority, self-possessed and uncompromising, of a man who could deal with anything that came his way.

Emma, who until that moment had considered herself to be confident and assured, despised the uncertain note in her voice as she said, 'Sorry to keep you waiting, but if I don't make him obey orders he'll grow up undisciplined.'

Coolly, inflexibly the stranger said, 'And for a Rottweiler that would be disastrous. I meant what I said. If I see him in my paddocks again I'll shoot him.'

Delivered calmly, it was a simple statement, not a threat. Emma knew perfectly well that any farmer in New Zealand had the right to shoot a dog that chased stock; nevertheless she had to block an unwise and impetuous response.

'And don't say he wouldn't worry sheep,' the man continued, not trying to soften the grimness in his voice. 'From chasing to killing is only a step.' He bent his head a little to examine the corgi, now sitting at Emma's feet. His voice hardened as he said, 'Usually it's the work of at least two dogs, one a bitch.'

'Babe is fourteen years old,' Emma retorted crisply. 'She can hardly stagger along the road.'

'I've seen older dogs than that bale up lambs and rip their throats out. Keep them both off my land.' Delivered in the same inexorable tone as everything else he'd said, there was no room for negotiation in the warning.

Emma nodded stiffly, grateful for once that she had long curling lashes, eminently suitable for hiding any resentful, mutinous expression in her grey eyes. She found herself staring at the exact place where a button fastened his checked shirt, revealing the tanned skin of his throat. Slow and steady, a pulse beat in the smooth hollow there.

A primal reaction—sharp and dangerous as a lightning spike to the ground—ripped through her. Lucky pressed against her from behind, and she put her hand down to his blunt head, stroking behind the ears while she tried to regain her composure.

Nothing, she thought dazedly, will ever be the same again. In some strange, terrifying way she'd been fundamentally changed—almost as though her basic cellular structure had been twisted and she'd been transformed into a different woman.

Oh, for heaven's sake!

Had she said the words or just thought them? Whatever, she was behaving like a schoolgirl imprisoned in the agony and exhilaration of her first crush.

It was his size, common sense soothed. He was big enough to be intimidating—bigger than enough, actually.

Then he moved slightly, so that the sun wasn't behind his head.

Told often enough that she was pretty, Emma had come to despise the word and its implications of softness and sweetness with all her heart, so she was normally unimpressed by outward appearances. Because she had big grey eyes and a soft red mouth, white skin with a delicate pink tinge, and because her black hair and lashes curled and shone, many people expected her to flirt and laugh and be light-hearted and docile and slightly stupid.

So she distrusted those who read character from the random mishmash of genetic inheritance that formed most faces. But this man's personality as revealed in his countenance hit her with the full-blown impact of an earthquake.

He certainly wasn't handsome. Beneath hair as black as

sorrow the strong framework of his face added authority to his powerful presence, a presence emphasised by blazing, remote, tawny eyes, keen and fierce and impersonal as those of a raptor.

Striking, her stunned mind supplied, trying to be helpful by using words to distance her from that first, mind-blowing shock. Oh, yes, he was striking—and impressive, and disturbing, forceful and dynamic. And a whole lot of other adjectives she couldn't think of just then because her brain had collapsed into curds.

In his thirties—old enough to set every one of her twenty-three years at naught—the stranger had a face defined by a blade of a nose and a jaw that took no prisoners.

And yet...

And yet, although his mouth was held straight by an uncompromising will, it was beautifully sculpted, and there was a probably deceptive fullness about the bottom lip. The man himself might make her think of a granite peak in a mountain range, bleak and stony and compelling, but in spite of the discipline he exerted on that chiselled mouth it hinted at caged emotions.

Interesting.

But not to her. Emma knew her limitations, and this man was so far beyond them she and he might as well inhabit different worlds.

He said, 'Those are Mrs Firth's dogs.'

'Yes.' It would serve him right, she thought, if she refused to answer his implied question, but one glance at the arrogant features and the cold fire of those eyes convinced her that discretion was the way to go. She added, 'I'm looking after them while she's in Canada.'

Straight dark brows drew together above the blade of his nose. 'At her daughter's?' After Emma's reluctant nod he pursued, 'When did she go?'

'Yesterday.'

'When will she be back?'

With frigid politeness Emma said, 'I'm afraid I don't know.'

'You must have some idea of how long you intend to stay here.'

Definitely not a subtle man. Emma's tone chilled further as she replied, 'Three weeks.'

'And you're wondering what business it is of mine.'

He might be nosy and unsubtle, but he wasn't stupid. She contented herself with a slight, dismissive smile.

'It's my business,' he said, in a voice that had dropped to a dangerous, silky quietness, 'because you can't control that Rottweiler. I'm Kane Talbot and those are my sheep he was chasing.'

Resisting the urge to wipe suddenly clammy hands down the side seams of her jeans, Emma said, 'I'm Emma Saunders, and from now on whenever we're near your sheep I'll keep Lucky on a leash.'

'Will you be able to manage him?' The fierce predator's gaze assessed her from the top of her curly head to her gumboots. 'You don't look strong enough.'

Every hair on her skin pulled tight. Furious at the involuntary reaction, Emma said woodenly, 'I'm stronger than I look, and Lucky walks well on a leash.' He didn't like it, but his sweet temper kept him obedient.

'I hope so.' After a taut, humming moment he ordered, 'And shut both of them up at night.'

'They are *always* locked up at night.'

Kane Talbot looked down his arrogant nose. 'Good.'

Pushing her luck, she said sweetly, 'Thank you. Come on, Lucky, Babe, we'll head for home.'

Straight black brows rose as the man's glance switched to the dogs at her feet. No doubt, she thought sarcastically, he called his sheepdogs names like Dig and Flo and Tip, good, practical names that could be heard over the noise of a flock of sheep and were easy to combine with swear words.

'I'll give you a lift,' he said. He was driving a Land

Rover, both dusty and mud-splashed, entirely suitable for dogs.

Formally, although not without a trace of relish in her tone, Emma replied, 'That's very kind of you, but the idea of the exercise is—well, exercise. We'll walk back.' She turned away, saying, 'Home, Babe. Home, Lucky.'

As she and the reluctant dogs marched back up the road she could feel the cold burn of his gaze on the back of her neck. Her shoulders stiffened until the sound of the engine told her that he was safely back in his Land Rover.

She knew where he lived. Right opposite Mrs Firth's house.

Oh, not in anything so ordinary as Mrs Firth's charming bungalow set in its acre of garden and orchard, with a lazy little stream running over an ancient lava flow at the bottom of the garden. No, Kane Talbot, who owned large chunks of New Zealand's northernmost peninsula, lived in a splendid house a mile or so from the road.

Kane Talbot, Mrs Firth had informed her, was old money and old influence; as well as holding a position of power on one of the big cooperative enterprises that ran the producer boards in New Zealand, he had varied business interests, moving easily between his life as one of New Zealand's most efficient and productive station owners and his wider urban and international interests.

Furthermore, he was suspected of being almost engaged to an Australian woman from an impeccable and influential family.

While they'd waited at Auckland airport for the plane to Vancouver Mrs Firth, a cryptic crossword addict who enjoyed searching out the meaning of words, had told Emma that the most probable derivation of his surname was the old French word *talebot*, meaning bandit.

'I'm not in the least surprised,' Emma observed beneath her breath now, waving briefly as the Land Rover went by with a sharp toot.

Once well past, Kane Talbot accelerated up the metal

road before turning onto a drive lined with huge magnolia trees, now coming into bloom. Just as no one could deny the pink and white fairytale glory of that avenue, it was impossible to deny the impact of its owner.

Whose first name, according to Mrs Firth, could be derived from the Welsh language. If so, it meant beautiful.

Emma grinned with involuntary enjoyment. Not likely!

On the other hand, if it came from the Manx language that was much more suitable because then it would mean warrior. And she could certainly see Kane Talbot as a warrior bandit. He exuded a no-holds-barred toughness, the hard, dynamic determination of a man who didn't know when to give up.

Recreating that autocratic face in her mind, she recalled the harsh moulding of chin and jaw and nose, the decisive authority that revealed itself in every line and angle and plane, and in the intelligent, icy fire of his eyes. He'd make a bad enemy.

Yet he had, she acknowledged reluctantly as she called Lucky to heel again, been surprisingly calm about the situation. Most farmers confronted by a dog clearly chasing sheep would have gone ballistic.

Odd, then, that his controlled detachment had set warning bells clashing.

Her mouth twisted. Her response was probably an atavistic relic from the days when a woman confronted by so much male presence packaged in well-honed muscles had had good reason to be wary.

'Lucky, heel!' she commanded forcefully, frowning at another male seething with presence and packaged in smoothly flowing muscles, with a strength of will almost as formidable as Kane Talbot's.

Oh, well, she knew how to handle dogs, and she wouldn't be seeing much of Kane Talbot.

And if Mrs Firth, who had let her charming pup get away with murder, was to be able to manage him when she got back from staying with her pregnant daughter, then Emma would have to teach Lucky that dogs who wanted to survive in the country didn't go chasing sheep.

She looked at his alert black and tan head and began to laugh quietly. Until that moment she hadn't realised that as well as attitude he and Kane Talbot were an almost identical match in colouring, with the same sable hair; the tawny markings of the Rottweiler were only slightly darker than the man's unusual eyes.

At least their black hair was sleek, not fluffy with curls like hers. Combine those curls with big grey eyes, fine, fragile skin, and a cupid's bow of a mouth, and what you got was a vapid, baby face. The fact that Emma knew why she was always being treated as though she were much younger than twenty-three didn't make it any easier to bear.

Oh, she was glad she wasn't ugly, but she'd like to have a face with some character to it.

Once home, she rubbed both dogs down and fed them, then went into the house and surveyed the contents of the refrigerator. Tomorrow she'd have to drive into Parahai and buy some more food.

She had just steered Mrs Firth's elderly silver Volvo through the gate when a large dark green car debouched onto the road from beneath the avenue of magnolias.

Overnight Emma had decided that her first impressions of Kane Talbot must have been coloured by her guilt about Lucky's behaviour. No man could possibly be so—well, so much!

It was a conclusion she revised now as he stopped, got out of the vehicle and strode across while she closed the gates behind Mrs Firth's car.

How could one man reduce the beauty around him to a mere accompaniment, Emma asked the universe crossly, his force of character effortlessly overpowering the natural loveliness of the valley?

Head erect, she waited at the car door while her pulses

skipped a beat. Remember that Australian almost-fiancée, she reminded herself sternly.

'Good morning.' Kane's tawny eyes examined her with a leisurely interest that lifted her hackles. 'The warrant of fitness on the Volvo is overdue.'

Brows drawn together, Emma swung around to peer at the windscreen. Sure enough, in the excitement of leaving Mrs Firth must have forgotten to have it renewed. 'I'll make an appointment to have it seen to,' she said, adding with rigid politeness, 'Thank you for pointing it out.'

He said negligently, 'I've got a cellphone in the car. Why not ask the garage if they'll do it today?'

'Well—thank you.'

She preferred, she thought as she accompanied him across the road, the man who had been so aloof yesterday. She didn't want neighbourly actions and consideration from Kane Talbot. He made her feel small and incompetent and—pretty.

After keying in a number he handed the phone to her, then moved a few steps away. He had good manners; she watched as he bent to examine some weed growing on the verge.

She blinked as a man's voice answered, and regrouped her scattered thoughts to explain to the mechanic what she wanted.

'OK,' he said. 'I'll try to do it today, but I haven't seen the car before so it might take a bit longer than usual.'

Emma frowned, then remembered that as Mrs Firth had only moved north a month ago the last warrant would have been issued in Taupo, a good six hours' drive southwards. Where, she thought feverishly, dragging her gaze away from the muscled contours of Kane's backside and thighs, she wished she was at this very moment. Except that Taupo was no longer her home.

She said, 'That's all right—I've got shopping to do.'

'OK, drop it off, then.'

Kane stood up. She handed the phone back and smiled

with what she hoped was cool and impersonal friendliness. 'Thank you,' she said again, ignoring Lucky's deep barking from inside the house.

'You've got ragwort growing on the verge,' he said crisply.

Emma bristled; she'd seen the bright yellow flowers in incompetent farmers' paddocks and was well aware that it was a vile pest, poisonous to sheep as well as smothering good grass. 'Where?'

He pointed out a small rosette of leaves. 'I'll send someone down to spray it.'

'I'll dig it out.'

'It would be a waste of time. In fact it would make matters worse because you can never get all the roots, and each one left in the ground sends up another shoot. Unfortunately spraying is the only way to kill it. Don't worry—it's as much to my advantage to see that it's dealt with as it is to Mrs Firth's. I don't want to have to conduct a mop-up operation on my own property.'

Emma's gaze flew to the paddocks on the other side of the road. Smooth and vigorously green, they had the opulent air of good husbandry.

'I don't suppose you do,' she said. 'Thank you. Mrs Firth will be very grateful when she comes back.'

'I gather you're house-sitting for her,' he said.

'Yes.' She smiled politely. 'Dog-sitting, really. Babe pines in kennels, and Mrs Firth thought this would be less stressful for her.'

'Obviously you know her well.'

He certainly chose the straightest and most direct route to get information. Whipping up resentment, because it smothered more complex emotions she didn't want to examine, Emma explained aloofly, 'Until Mrs Firth came up here she lived next door to me.'

'So you're from Taupo.'

'Yes.' She was not going to tell him that Taupo was no

longer her home; when she left Parahai she'd be going to a new job and a new life in Hamilton.

'And how do you enjoy being nanny to a couple of dogs?' he asked, smiling.

Amusement turned his eyes to pure, glinting gold, Emma registered dazedly. And that smile! Although it didn't soften the hard framework of his face, it transformed his powerful male charisma into a potent sexuality.

'Very much,' she said, using the words to distract her from the intensity of her response. 'Babe's a darling, and Lucky—well, Rottweilers are very determined animals, so they need guidance and firm training, otherwise they believe they're the leaders of the pack. Then they can become dangerous because they see their job as protecting the others in the pack and enforcing discipline. Lucky has to understand that in his pack he's down at the bottom. He takes orders; he doesn't give them.'

'Can you make him do that?'

At the note of scepticism in his question, Emma lifted her round chin. 'Yes,' she said with complete confidence. 'As any nanny will tell you, it's just a matter of training and praise, training and praise until eventually he gets the idea.'

'And what training do *you* have for this?' he asked, looking down at her with unreadable eyes.

'I'm a registered vet nurse,' she told him coolly, 'and I've done a lot of work with a man who breeds dogs for obedience trials. I've known Lucky since he was six weeks old, and I can handle him because he really wants to please me.'

'I'm not surprised,' he said, his voice somehow goading.

Acutely and suspiciously aware of the breeze lifting her curls, the sun's golden caress on her skin, the way the light emphasised the rugged strength of Kane Talbot's features, Emma said, 'Dogs usually do want to please,' trying to cut off the conversation without making it seem obvious.

Foolishly, she looked him straight in the eyes.

She'd heard the clichés—'my heart stood still,' friends had told her, or, 'I sizzled right down to my toes.'

She'd never thought to experience that sort of reaction to any man. Yet when she met Kane Talbot's gaze she fell headfirst into topaz fire; alien sensations scorched down her backbone and she stiffened at the clutch of an unbidden hunger in the pit of her stomach.

Mercifully, a renewed fusillade of barks from the house dragged her back from that dangerous brink.

Twisting away, she blinked several times at the silver hood of Mrs Firth's car to clear her sight. 'I'd better get going,' she said—how strange that her voice was perfectly steady—'before Lucky decides to break a window to rescue me.'

It was a stupid thing to say, and to his credit Kane didn't pick her up on it. Instead he said, 'One day you must tell me how he managed to acquire a name like that.'

She slid into the car, realising only when she'd finished clicking on the seatbelt that he held the door for her. 'I'll do that,' she said, nodding at a point just over his left shoulder.

'If you wait, I'll go ahead and show you the way to the garage.'

A little too sharply she countered, 'That's very kind of you, but if you tell me where it is you won't need to bother.' She managed to produce a smile. 'It must be difficult to get lost in Parahai.'

'Impossible. Turn left at the crossroads. The workshop is on the right about three hundred metres past it.'

'Thank you.'

Her breath sighed out as he closed the door and stood back to let her drive on.

Accelerating down the road, she thought with real gratitude that she wasn't likely to see much of him. According to Mrs Firth he had interests in Australia and North America, so he was often out of the country.

Which was just as well, because he didn't appear to be

attacked by the same treacherous weakness that still quickened her pulses. His hard, angular face hadn't changed, and there'd been no answering glitter in the glacial depths of those eyes. Naturally, because he was in love with another woman. Since all of her friends who had fallen in lust had assured her that it was mutual, a meeting of desires across a crowded room, this had to be a crush rather than lust. She'd get over it.

And it had better happen soon, she thought, noticing that his car was already in her rearview mirror. Apart from anything else, the physical manifestations were embarrassing and extravagant.

And scary. She'd never realised she could feel like this—as though the world and all her interests had suddenly condensed to an unbearable focus on one man. Exciting it certainly was, but far from comfortable.

Not to mention the fact that she was much too busy to waste time developing a hopeless crush on someone at least ten years older than she was, and light-years ahead of her in sophistication. Who belonged to another woman.

Setting her jaw, she drove sedately for ten minutes through farms and orchards, finally coming down a steep hill to the village. Parahai was a small town on the edge of a narrow, winding inlet. Once a busy coastal shipping port and now a yachting haven, it served a diverse area of farms and stations and orchards. Because there were beaches close by it was a holiday town, so during summer the tree-lined streets were probably frantic.

In spring it was laid back enough to be friendly, and that holiday rush ensured that the shops were of a higher standard than she'd expected in such a small place. Emma liked the ambience, admired the pohutukawa trees shading the main street, and enjoyed the quick smiles of the locals.

She followed Kane's directions to the workshop and got out, tensing as his car drew up beside her. Leaning into the Volvo, she pulled out her bag and asked sweetly as she straightened, 'Have you discovered that your warrant is overdue too?'

He got out—all long legs and shoulders, she thought crossly—and surveyed her with tawny eyes iced by mockery. 'No.'

Quelling the urge to be very rude, Emma headed towards the workshop. He caught her up within two strides.

The owner looked up as they walked in. 'Hi, Kane,' he said amiably, 'I didn't know you were coming in today.' But that's all right, his tone revealed.

Kane introduced him to Emma, who had to suffer the open interest in the man's eyes as he said, 'Yep, fine, no problem. She should be done in a couple of hours, no sweat.'

Clearly, having Kane with her made her someone to be reckoned with, Emma decided irritably. In spite of his easy-going attitude, there was no mistaking the mechanic's respect. She handed over the keys and he got into the Volvo and drove it into the workshop.

Kane said, 'I'll drop you off wherever you want to go.'

It wasn't actually a suggestion. With a small, acid pleasure Emma said, 'If you don't mind I'll walk into town. I'd like to look at the gardens on the way and it's not far.'

No doubt her smile was as insincere as her excuse, because the dark brows drew together for a second and heavy eyelids masked the topaz glitter of his gaze before he said evenly, 'Of course. But you should wear a hat. Spring comes early up here and the sun can burn any time of the year.'

His eyes lingered a moment on the fine, pale skin of her face, bringing heat flaring to the surface.

'I'll remember that,' she said primly, and set off down the road. Arrogant oaf!

Well, no, 'oaf' was the wrong word. He wore clothes that had been made for him by a very good tailor, and there was nothing provincial about him at all; he possessed a worldliness and self-assurance that was all the more potent for being entirely unconscious.

And beneath it there was strength and something predatory, something untamed and battle-hardened, she thought, walking briskly up the road.

Now where had that idea come from?

From the man himself. He had a warrior's discipline, a power based on cold, unemotional courage and expertise.

And that, Emma scoffed, ignoring a particularly colourful garden, was pure imagination! He possessed a natural male magnetism that attracted a woman's interest, and she could tell by his muscles that he worked hard, but, although she was certain he could handle himself in any situation, he wasn't a superhero. They didn't exist. She'd simply been overwhelmed by an excess of pure male charisma.

And everyone knows, she thought with a faint, malicious smile, that charisma has nothing to do with character—it's a fairy godmother's doting gift, handed to the unworthy as well as the good.

The big green car passed her with almost no sound beyond a little toot that irritated her even more; setting her chin, she strode down the footpath, examining magnolias and camellias and daffodils with a determined interest.

Kane had been right when he'd said spring came early in the north; the daffodils were in full glory, daphne bushes perfumed the air with their sharp, exquisite scent, the poplar-like cherry trees she'd noticed were ablaze with tiny rosy-cerise bells, and freesias and annuals mingled in bright profusion in every flowerbed.

Clearly no gardener in Parahai worried about late frosts.

The walk calmed her, so that by the time Emma got to the village she was ready to enjoy its atmosphere. First she called into the bank, to make sure that everything was under control with her account, and then she spent a very pleasant hour acquainting herself with the stock in both the bookshop and a small boutique that specialised in chic, casual clothes.

Nice, but too expensive, she thought, eyeing a smart pair of capri pants with a matching shirt and waistcoat in the crisp, clear grey that suited her. The move from her flat in Taupo to a unit in Hamilton, a bustling city some distance away, had drained more from her bank balance than she'd budgeted for. As she didn't start her new job for three weeks, she'd have to be careful with her savings.

She found the local library and organised a temporary membership before choosing a detective novel set in ancient Rome and a big, fat historical novel written by a woman who was both a scholar and a brilliant author. Though Mrs Firth had many books, they were mostly about gardening and cooking; Emma enjoyed them, but wanted a little variety.

After that she sat out a shower in a coffee bar that overlooked a little courtyard, where a fountain spilled a shimmer of water over three graduated cockle shells and more flowers bloomed in pots, mostly big, blowzy pansies in shades of blue and purple and yellow. Smiling over her coffee cup at the antics of the sparrows outside, Emma let her irritation fade.

No doubt Kane Talbot didn't intend to be so autocratic. He'd probably been born that way, she thought, and grinned at the image of a small baby with that imperious nose and chin bending an entire household to his will.

Finally she went to the supermarket, buying the staples she needed before allowing herself the pleasure of choosing a few mandarins, cushiony and glowing, a dark purplish-green avocado and some smooth, ruby, egg-shaped tamarillos, her favourite fruit, so frost-tender they only survived where winters were mild and short.

Leaving the bags to be called for, she set off for the garage again, enjoying the salt-tanged, sunlit air and the huge white clouds that sailed rapidly across the bright sky.

She was a few minutes early, but the mechanic had finished. Wiping his hands on a piece of cloth, he said, 'I can't give you a warrant, Ms Saunders, because she needs a new clutch plate. You must have noticed she was shuddering a bit when you started.'

'Oh,' Emma said blankly. 'Well, yes, but I thought it was just because the car was old.'

'She's a dowager, all right, but she's in great heart and a new clutch plate will make all the difference,' he said encouragingly.

Emma asked the probable cost, and frowned at his reply. 'That's a lot of money,' she said. 'I'll have to—'

And stopped, because he glanced past her as someone joined them.

'Trouble?' Kane Talbot asked.

The garage owner explained again, and Kane said calmly, 'That's all right. We'll leave the car here and Emma can contact Mrs Firth when she gets home.' He switched that hard-edged glance to her. 'If Mrs Firth agrees to the repairs, ring Joe before five this afternoon and he'll get the part couriered up from Auckland tonight. That way you'll have the car back almost as soon as if you told him to go ahead now.'

'Yep, that's right,' the mechanic said cheerfully.

Aware that her reluctance to do this was based entirely on the fact that it was Kane who'd suggested it, Emma nodded. 'OK,' she said to the mechanic. 'I'll contact you as soon as I've rung Mrs Firth.'

'Fine.' The mechanic nodded at Kane before going back into the workshop.

Emma stood quite still, battling a chill, empty feeling as though somehow the ground had been neatly cut from under her feet.

'Have you left parcels somewhere?' Kane asked.

'At the supermarket.'

'Right, we'll go and get them.'

Because there was nothing else to do she went with him, accepting the unforced politeness that put her into the passenger's seat. He obviously didn't care whether she *wanted* him to extend such courtesies to her—he performed them automatically. After a rapid glance Emma decided that he'd probably never even heard of political correctness or the feminist movement.

She felt, she told herself crisply, sorry for that woman in Australia.

The seats were leather and very comfortable. Emma folded her hands in her lap and looked down at them. The seatbelt fitting snugly across her chest seemed to be blocking her breath. Deliberately she inhaled, but barely had time to fill her lungs before Kane opened the door and got in behind the wheel.

CHAPTER TWO

'ENJOY your morning?' Kane asked as he turned the key.

'Yes, thank you.'

'It's a nice little town.' He changed gear and inclined his dark head to someone who'd tooted and waved from another car. 'How did that Rottweiler get its name? Lucky is all right for a sheepdog or a Labrador, but it's no name for a guard dog.'

Emma was halfway through her answer before she remembered that she'd planned to stay stiff and distant all the way home. By then it was too late, so she kept on going in her usual pleasant voice.

'He was lucky Mrs Firth came to collect Babe from the clinic I worked for in Taupo. Or perhaps he was lucky Babe chased a roaming goat out of Mrs Firth's garden and hurt her paw. She stayed in the clinic overnight, and while she was there a man brought Lucky in. He'd been given the pup but his wife thought it would grow into a monster that might eat their children, so he dumped it on us. When Mrs Firth came to pick up Babe the pup was in a cage, bawling his head off.'

'And she couldn't resist him.' He sounded amused and a little patronising.

A swift glance from beneath her lashes revealed that he was smiling. No doubt *he* never did anything on impulse.

Looking straight ahead, Emma said woodenly, 'When she went over to say hello, Lucky rushed across and pressed his face into her hand as though she'd been sent to rescue him.'

Kane laughed quietly. 'Did he do that to you too?'

'Oh, yes, but I didn't tell Mrs Firth that. He was going to be put down, you see.'

'Not exactly good pet material,' he observed. 'They're tough dogs, and they need a lot of work to keep them happy.'

'Corgis might look very sweet, but they're tough dogs too, and Mrs Firth trained Babe well enough.' This was stretching the point; although Babe was devoted to her mistress, and more than amiable with Emma, she was inclined to snap at strangers, and she certainly ruled the roost in the house.

'You can pick a corgi up if it misbehaves,' Kane said ironically.

Emma shrugged. 'Rottweilers are good, even-tempered dogs if they're taught properly. They're really clever—they remember almost everything. I think Lucky's playfulness and exuberance comes from his grandmother, who was a boxer. His jumping ability certainly does. He'll be fine.'

She hoped she sounded convincing.

The car slid into the supermarket car park. Kane Talbot got out and so did she, walking quickly inside to pick up her parcels. Again he caught her up before she'd taken more than a few steps.

It was, she thought a few moments later, rather like being with royalty. He knew everybody; they knew him. He greeted people as they walked through the shop, meeting smiles and interested glances. But he didn't stop to introduce anyone. And he scooped up her three plastic bags without asking whether she needed any help.

The sort of man who simply took over, Emma thought, replacing a quirk of resentment with resignation. Good in emergencies, but unbearable in everyday life. That poor woman in Australia—after a year of marriage she wouldn't have a thought to call her own.

Back in the car, groceries safely stowed, he switched on the engine and asked casually, 'Do you ride?'

After a moment's pause she said, 'Yes.'

'I have a mare that badly needs exercise. I'm too big for her and no one's been on her for a couple of months.'

'You don't know whether I'm any good,' she said.

When his tawny glance flicked across her hands, the fingers curled. She felt as though she'd been branded.

'I think you'll be all right,' he said with cool, abrasive confidence, 'but if you sit like a sack of spuds and saw at her mouth I'll rescind the offer.'

Surprised into a short laugh, she said, 'All right, I'd like to try her out.'

'She's not placid.'

'Neither am I,' Emma said dulcetly.

Something glittered beneath the long black lashes. 'No? You look as sweet and demure as a good child.'

Slowly, with great effort, Emma relaxed her hands until they rested sedately in her lap. She'd like to hit him fair and square in the middle of that flat stomach, right on the solar plexus so that she winded him, so that he doubled up and gasped and had to wipe tears from those brilliant eyes.

Restraining the sudden and most unusual surge of anger, she looked down unseeingly. She'd probably break every knuckle if she tried to punch him, and besides, he didn't look as though he'd accept an attack with equanimity. She stifled the quick, sly query from some hidden part of her brain about how he'd deal with a woman's aggression, carefully smoothed her brow and leashed her imagination with a strong will.

He probably didn't mean to sound patronising—and then she looked up and caught the narrow gleam of gold in his eyes and knew that he damned well did.

She produced a smile. 'I know,' she said with a sigh. 'I look like Snow White. That wretched film's blighted my life.'

'You wouldn't have let the wicked stepmama drive you out into the snow?'

How did—? No, he couldn't know! Colour seeped back into her suddenly clammy skin. When she'd been sixteen she'd fought her prospective stepmother with the only weapon she'd had, her father's love, and she'd won. Now, seven years too late, she regretted it bitterly.

Fighting to keep her voice even, she said, 'No. As for housekeeping for seven miners—never.'

'And I don't suppose you're just hanging about waiting for the prince to ride by on his white horse?'

'Give her credit,' she retorted, 'she was in a coma—she couldn't actually go out looking for him.'

'True,' he said, and ruthlessly dragged the conversation back to the subject. 'So you don't intend to be any man's reward?'

'If we're still talking about Snow White,' she returned, 'don't you think that the prince was *her* reward? She'd put up with a lot, worked hard for years and fought off a couple of murderous attacks before succumbing to treachery, and then along came this nice young man who apparently believed in love at first sight. She deserved a treat, and he was it.'

He laughed. 'Perhaps you're right. Interesting—fairy stories read as feminist fables.'

'Nothing as intellectual and rigorous,' Emma said firmly. 'It's just that I got called Snow White so often that I had to develop some sort of attitude to the wretched thing.'

'I'll bet you were a tomboy.'

The arrogant, angular profile showed no emotion at all, but the corner of his mouth tucked up. It irritated her that he could read her so easily, and behind that chagrin flickered fear.

Men, Emma had discovered, didn't really understand women. Seven years ago her father had refused to believe that his daughter was lying and cheating with one aim only: to smash his relationship with the woman he'd been having an affair with, the woman he planned to marry. Because Emma had never been rude, never thrown down any gauntlet, always been polite, he'd believed her and allowed himself to be manipulated by her feigned bulimia.

Looking back down the years, she shivered with dismay as she recalled how grimly she'd battled with the woman she'd believed to be a greedy, unprincipled interloper. Rage and grief had fuelled her determination. She hadn't cared that her father had truly loved his mistress; she'd been determined to punish them for being lovers while her mother, made wretched by their affair, had suffered and died.

Punish them Emma had. Her father had sent his lover away, and—completely taken in by her pretence—devoted himself to getting Emma through her illness.

A year later he'd died of a heart attack. Sometimes, when she lay awake in the voiceless night, she wondered whether he'd have lived if she hadn't taken it on herself to avenge his betrayal of her mother, if she hadn't in turn betrayed her father by lying and cheating. The irony of her own behaviour was now very clear to her.

Kane Talbot seemed a lot more perceptive than most men. Those amber eyes, lit by a clear ring of gold around the dark centres, saw more than she liked.

More acidly than she'd intended, she replied, 'Turning into a tomboy is the classic response to looking like Snow White. I climbed the highest trees, rode the toughest horses, broke arms and skinned knees galore, and had to prove myself over and over again.'

'The onset of adolescence must have been a shock,' he observed.

'Isn't it to everyone?' Emma asked with offhand insouciance. 'A friend of mine, a thin, shy redhead, was always the tallest in the class—everyone called her Legs. She got unmercifully teased all through primary school. At fifteen she shot up to almost six feet, developed a face to stun the angels, and is now one of the world's top models.'

And Emma would bet a considerable sum of money that Kane had never had any problems with growing up—or with anything, unless it was swatting away women. That indefinable thing called star quality had probably been obvious from the moment he'd first smiled in his cradle.

Except that 'star' was a lightweight description, and there was nothing lightweight about Kane Talbot. The quality that made him immediately noticeable was based on calm mastery of his strength and dynamic power.

Of course, growing up heir to large amounts of money helped. People respected power and influence.

And even as that last snide comment popped into her brain she discarded it. Whatever situation Kane Talbot had been born into he'd still possess that air of authority and courage. It was innate.

Kane broke into her thoughts with, 'And do you envy this top model?'

'Good heavens, no.' She thought a moment, then added fairly, 'Well, the money would be nice, but I'd go crazy leaping around like they have to, not to mention the hours it takes to make up their faces and do their hair. Sorrel's into meditation and poetry, so she just lets it all wash over her while she thinks out her next poem, or communes with the infinite, or whatever you do when you meditate. She's giving it until she's thirty, and then she's going to retire and write the great New Zealand novel, which she's sure is going to be difficult enough to keep her interested and striving for the rest of her life.'

'She sounds interesting herself,' he said.

Emma gave a mental shrug. 'She is,' she said sturdily. All men were intrigued by beautiful women; why be surprised—and, yes, disappointed—that he fitted the pattern?

He slowed, and turned into the gateway of Mrs Firth's house. 'I can hear the dogs barking from here,' he said.

'Babe never used to bark until Lucky arrived,' Emma told him. 'She taught him his manners, and he taught her that a dog is supposed to raise the roof whenever a stranger appears.'

'And is she the leader of the pack?'

'Well, she's above him,' she said, relaxing. 'And I'm above them both, although I do have to keep reminding them that I'm top dog. Lucky is sure we females need protecting, and Babe thinks I'm a snippety young upstart who needs to be taught a few manners myself.'

Absurdly pleased at his laughter, she waited until he'd stopped to say, 'I'll get out here and then we won't have to open and shut the gate.'

'All right,' he said pleasantly. 'I'll carry your parcels in.'

Emma sighed silently and got out. She needed fresh air to banish the sound of that low, amused laugh and calm her jittery heartbeat. 'I'll let the dogs out,' she called, and walked smartly up the drive to the back door. Both dogs bounded out, although Babe stayed with Emma. Lucky, however, raced barking down towards the car and the open gate.

'Sit,' Kane said in a voice that held no fear and no apprehension of disobedience.

The dog skidded to a halt, then obeyed the repeated command and sat. Looking slightly bewildered, he stared up at Kane, who waited a moment to establish dominance, then held out his hand. Lucky made to rise, was bade sternly to sit again, and obeyed instantly. He sniffed Kane's long fingers with interest and respect, then gazed up into his face. It was ridiculous, but Emma felt shut out from a purely masculine moment.

'Stay away from my sheep,' Kane said sternly.

Lucky's tail, long because Mrs Firth didn't approve of docking, swept the ground.

Kane said, 'How do you release him?'

'G-o-o-d b-o-y.'

He said the words and Lucky sprang up, eagerly sniffing around the car, getting ready to cock his leg until both Emma and Kane said 'No' sharply enough to make him look startled and back off.

'Two nannies,' Kane said with an ironic smile. 'He'll develop a complex.'

A sudden glow in Emma's heart shocked her. Instinct warned her that Kane Talbot was not good medicine for inexperienced women. Although Emma enjoyed challenges, some, she knew, were not worth the exhilaration.

She and Kane had nothing in common. He was cosmopolitan, with a sophistication that was so essential a part of him he probably didn't even realise he possessed it. Not for him the fake worldliness, the desperate effort to be cool of so many younger men. And he was almost engaged, whatever that meant.

Watching the broad shoulders flex as he hoisted the grocery bags from the boot, Emma thought that he'd know exactly how to make a woman so aware of him she'd begin to think of all sorts of disturbing things, like how good he'd be as a lover.

A disconcerting wrench of sensation in her stomach turned to heat. Fortunately he was so much older than her—ten years or so, she guessed—that he probably did think of her as barely grown up. He was just being a considerate neighbour; she was the one with the problem.

'Here, I'll take a bag,' she said, when it was obvious he intended to carry all three in.

'They're not heavy.'

Setting her jaw, she followed him up the two steps to the brick porch at the back of the house. She didn't realise that he'd stood back to let her go first until she cannoned into him.

'Ouff,' she muttered, leaping back with a memory of muscles like iron and a faint, sexy scent, not soap or shaving lotion, just Kane Talbot.

'Sorry,' he said calmly.

She gave him a brief glance, and muttered as she went in, 'I didn't see you.'

Leading the way into the kitchen, she took a couple of deep breaths to centre herself. 'Just put them on the bench, please,' she said, pointing to the smooth grey granite.

He did that, then glanced at her with amusement glinting beneath black lashes as straight as his brows.

Emma looked past him and said softly, 'Oh, look outside—on the maple branch. A tui!'

The iridescent bird ducked and bowed along the branch, head held low as he sang a soft, seductive song. At his throat a tuft of white feathers bobbed like a stock in a lace collar when he fluffed his wings and repeated the sinuous movements and his song. Against the glowing red stems of the maple tree he looked superb.

'What's he doing?' Emma asked quietly.

'He's courting.' Kane's voice was unexpectedly abrupt. 'He knows how splendidly those branches set off his colours; he's parading, looking for a mate, promising that he'll give her ecstasy and young ones and keep all their bellies filled.'

A note in his words dragged her gaze from the bird strutting his stuff outside. Kane's face had hardened into indifference, but there was a twist to his lips that gave his comment a satirical inflection.

Tentatively she asked, 'Would you like a cup of tea or coffee?'

'No, thank you, I have to keep going,' he said, the words so quick and cool they were a rebuff.

Brows pleated, Emma watched the big car go down the road and turn into his drive. He'd been reasonably friendly, and then suddenly, as though she'd insulted his mother, he'd withdrawn behind an impervious armour.

'Perhaps he thought I was flirting with him,' she told the dogs, who were eyeing the packets of pet mince with anticipatory interest. 'Well, he was wrong. Men with dangerous eyes and tough faces and volatile moods do nothing for me at all. Even when they're not virtually engaged to Australian women of impeccable family. Whoa, hold your horses; I'll make your dog biscuits this afternoon. I want to do some weeding first while it's fine.'

Once outside, Babe found a warm place on the brick terrace and went to sleep, while Lucky investigated a score of fascinating scents around the garden before settling close to her. As Emma tugged at weeds encouraged into growth by the warm touch of spring, she decided that her unexpected holiday had altered direction. Kane's arrival on the scene had sent her stumbling blindly into perilous, intriguing, unknown territory.

She yanked out a large sowthistle, patted back into place the three pansies its roots had dislodged, and tried to persuade herself that the slow excitement that licked through her whenever she thought of the man next door was uncomplicated attraction, a pragmatic indication from her genes that she was old enough to reproduce and that for the survival of her offspring it would be wise to choose a tough man who was a good provider, with enough prestige to protect her from other men as well as the strength to beat off cave bears and sabretooth tigers.

Basic stuff, an inheritance from the primitive past, still powerful even though it was outdated at the end of the twentieth century.

'And don't forget,' she reminded herself, 'the almost-fiancée.'

After an hour of solid work she stood to admire a bed of pansies and tall bluebells unmarred by weeds. But as she scrubbed the dirt from her fingernails she admitted that her next door neighbour had been constantly on her mind, disturbing her usually serene thoughts and refusing to go away.

The telephone rang. She scrabbled to dry her hands on the towel and ran into the kitchen. 'Yes?' she asked breathlessly.

'Were you outside?'

Divorced from the actual physical presence of the man, Kane Talbot's voice made its own impression. Deep and level, with an intriguing rasp in the middle register, it brushed across her skin like velvet.

'I was washing my hands,' she said, trying to sound cheerful and bright and ordinary. 'I've been weeding.'

'I thought Mrs Firth had Fran Partridge to help in the garden.'

'She does, but Ms Partridge went away this morning, and anyway, I like weeding.' Fran Partridge was a single mother and the probable source, Emma had decided on meeting her, of Mrs Firth's information about the locals.

How did she know Kane was frowning when he said, 'Where's Fran gone?'

A subtle undernote in his voice betrayed his expression. Before she'd realised it was none of his business, Emma told him, 'It's the school holidays and she's on a trip somewhere with her son.'

'Of course. I'd forgotten.' He was silent, possibly thinking of Davy Partridge, who lived at the end of the road and rode his bike up and down on fine days, singing at the top of his voice. 'It's unusual for someone of your age to be interested in gardening.'

Emma bristled. 'Is it?'

'Most twenty-year-olds prefer to be out and raving.' An ambiguous note of—amusement?—echoed through his words.

Emma's teeth clenched for a second on her bottom lip. 'Well, perhaps because I'm twenty-three instead of twenty, I enjoy gardening.'

'Ah, a mature woman.'

Definitely mockery. Her chin lifted. Very clearly she said, 'That, I suppose, is a matter of opinion. To someone of your age I might appear quite green and raw.'

'Sweet, actually,' he said odiously. 'Eleven years is enough to make us different generations. Do you want me to ring Mrs Firth and tell her what the problem with the car is?'

Didn't he trust her to be able to dial a number in Canada? Or did he think she was incapable of understanding the inner workings of an engine? Well, Emma thought, I've got news for you, Mr Talbot, *sir*. Lords of the manor have had their day; nowadays the peasants are more than capable of running their own lives.

Calmly she said, 'That's very kind, but it'll be all right. I'm sure she has some idea of how the car works and the terminology won't throw her. Or me,' she added dulcetly.

There was a moment's pause until he said in an amused voice, 'That's put me well and truly into my place.'

'I—'

He cut in, 'One thing I didn't say before—if you need anything, let me know. We pull together in the country; it makes life easier for all of us. Goodbye.' And he hung up.

'And goodbye to you, sir, Mr Talbot,' Emma said, crashing the receiver down. Lucky's tail swept the floor.

Laughing a little to blunt the raw intensity of her feelings, she said, 'Takes a dominant male to know one! Kane Talbot might be used to running everyone's lives around here but he's not going to run ours. We'd better go out and do some work together, Lucky. By the time your mistress comes back I'd like to have you able to stare at a sheep without wanting to chase it, which means you need to practise those commands. And, speaking of Mrs Firth, I'd better ring her right now and see what she wants done with her car.'

Next morning the sun was shining, and although the wind from the south was cold it had polished the sky into the radiant silvery blue that spring claims as its own. Yawning, Emma drew back the curtains and scanned the green, lovely contours of hill and valley.

Mrs Firth had given her permission to order a new clutch plate for the Volvo, so the part should be in Parahai by now. Thinking of that telephone call, Emma smiled. She'd had to field a couple of enquiries about Kane Talbot.

'A very sexy man, isn't he?' the older woman asked slyly.

'If you like them rough-edged and masterful,' Emma parried.

'Ah, I've seen him in evening clothes—no sign of rough edges then! You young things might like your idols to be pretty, but as you get older you appreciate the value of strength and power and discipline. He has a charming mother too.'

'It doesn't seem possible,' Emma said delicately.

'I'd like to see you both in action.' Mrs Firth laughed. 'I must go, Emma. Thank you so much for helping me in my hour of need. I'll never forget it, and neither will Philippa.'

Philippa was her daughter, five years older than Emma, and as Emma had already asked after her she knew that her pregnancy was not being an easy one.

'I had the free time,' Emma said cheerfully, 'and it's no hardship to spend it in a place like this, I promise you! Northland in the spring is glorious.'

Halfway through the morning, while she was drinking coffee out on the terrace, she said sternly, 'Sit!' to Lucky, and waited for him to decide not to race across the lawn and bark fearsomely at the car pulling into the gateway. He obeyed, but he did bark.

Tamping down a flicker of excitement, Emma ordered, 'Stay.'

Whining, he obeyed, and she left him to walk across the green damp lawn.

But it was not the car of yesterday, nor the Land Rover, and the driver, although tall, was nothing like the man who had managed to make himself so at home in her mind that she knew the exact shade of his eyes: a mixture of gold and bronze and flickering tawny fire that somehow chilled his gaze instead of heating it.

The woman leaning on the gate smiled at her, and as Emma was telling herself sturdily that she wasn't disappointed she recognised the smile.

'Hello,' Kane Talbot's mother said, 'I'm Felicity Talbot, and you are Emma Saunders, and over there, looking desperate, is L-u-c-k-y, whose name I will not say in case it persuades him to disobey you and come across.'

How could Kane Talbot have such a laughing, lovely mother? Emma shook the hand offered to her and agreed, 'It would indeed, and I shouldn't push him too far. Do you like dogs?'

'I love animals.'

So Emma said, 'Good boy, Lucky. Here.'

Even he fell for that charm. After hurtling across to the gate, he smelt Mrs Talbot's extended hand and gave her a swift swipe with his tongue before settling back on his haunches and beaming at her.

'What a darling,' she cooed.

'Your son didn't think so when he drove past as Lucky was chasing his sheep,' Emma said stringently.

Dark eyes widened. 'Goodness, it's a wonder he didn't shoot him then and there. Kane doesn't usually hand out second chances.'

It figured. 'I don't suppose he had a gun with him, so Lucky was—well, lucky. And he came back when I called him,' Emma explained. 'Kane was angry, but I promised most faithfully not to let the dog off a leash again whenever we went near sheep.'

'I should hope not! He looks as though he's biddable.'

'He's very teachable.' Emma turned as Babe woke up and realised they'd been joined by a stranger. Barking, she hobbled down from the terrace and sniffed her way across the lawn.

Stooping to let her smell her fingers, Kane's mother asked, 'Is she blind?'

'Not quite, but her eyes are failing. She hates being put in kennels, which is why I'm here. I've always looked after her when Mrs Firth's gone away. And Lucky had such a traumatic experience at the vet's when he was a puppy that he goes to pieces in any sort of institutional place.'

Mrs Talbot gave the corgi a final pat and straightened. 'How lucky for Mrs Firth that you could take over for her.'

She gave a charming smile. 'I haven't come to interfere with your day at all, but to ask if you'd like to come up to dinner at our place tomorrow night. It's just a little dinner, no fuss at all, and you'll meet some of the neighbours.'

Emma did not want to socialise with Kane Talbot, but it would be nice to meet the neighbours. So she smiled and replied, 'I'd love to, thank you very much.'

'Good. Around seven? I'll get someone to come down and pick you up.'

'No, no, I can walk up.'

Mrs Talbot looked startled. 'You'll get your shoes dirty. It's no problem.'

Clearly one did not attend a dinner party at the Talbots' place with dirty shoes, or even carry a pair to change into. Emma said, 'I'll drive up, then.'

'I thought the car was in dock?'

Emma said, 'It should be ready by tomorrow night.'

Unfortunately it wasn't. Emma, now dressed neatly in a silk shirtdress of black with a soft violet pattern, had had every intention of donning gumboots and walking, but late in the afternoon Kane had rung and told her laconically that he'd pick her up at seven.

Emma had opened her mouth to protest, then shrugged and agreed. She'd have graciously accepted any other offer of a lift; it was only because it was Kane that she wanted to assert her independence.

He arrived exactly on time and in a downpour of rain. Warned by barking, Emma raced from the bedroom, grabbed her umbrella and shot out through the front door, closing it carefully behind her. She'd had a last-minute battle with the strap of her slip—it tore from the bodice as she put it on and had to be anchored with a safety pin—but she met Kane with a smile and her best social manner.

'Good evening,' he said, taking her umbrella and holding a much larger one over her.

In one swift, startled glance Emma understood what Mrs Firth had meant. Kane looked as completely at home in the well-cut trousers and fine cotton shirt as he'd looked in the working clothes she'd first seen on him—not a rough edge in sight.

Of course his tailor had a good frame to work on. Kane's lithe, perfectly proportioned body enhanced anything he wore, but more than that, his powerful male potency reduced his clothes to mere accessories, carefully chosen and then forgotten.

'Hello,' Emma said, pretending that her heart was ambling along in its normal unnoticeable fashion. Rain hurtled against the roof of the house, and she raised her voice to ask, 'Do you want to wait until it goes over?'

'No. Guests will be arriving soon, and I need to be there when they come.' He looked down at the narrow-heeled shoes she wore. 'Would you like me to carry you out to the car?'

'No,' she said firmly as heat burnt across her cheeks. She peered out at the rain, driving in curtains of silver through the brilliant glow of the security lights, then said desperately, 'I think it's easing up,' and set off towards the car.

He got there before her and opened the door with one strong, negligent hand.

While she did up the seatbelt she watched him walk around to the other side. He didn't waste time or effort, moving with an economical, spare grace that liquefied her spine, and when he got in beside her the muscles in his thigh flexed beneath the superb cloth of his trousers. Swiftly, precisely, he put the car into gear, long-fingered hands casually competent.

Emma's pulse began to throb in her throat. On the way back from Parahai the other day it hadn't occurred to her that only a few centimetres separated her thigh from his; nothing had changed, so why was she so aware of it now?

She stared out at the avenue of magnolias, big, swooping trees holding their splendid flowers up to the dark sky.

When they fell the petals would carpet the vivid grass in pink and white for two weeks of exquisite beauty...

And because the silence in the car stretched and simmered with tension, she said, 'Those trees are a magnificent sight. Who planted them?'

'My parents, when my mother came here as a bride.'

Emma said, 'She must delight in them now.'

'Yes.'

'Will the rain spoil the flowers?'

'No.'

All right then, she thought, irritated rather than hurt by his abruptness, you can come up with the next subject of conversation.

The drive swooped past paddocks where large red cattle placidly chewed cuds in the sudden exposure of the headlights, then it branched and almost immediately a cattle-stop rattled under their wheels. Skilfully placed lighting illuminated a pond large enough to be called a lakelet. Framed by trees and gardens, it glimmered in the dusk and then was left behind as they drove beneath more trees and between wide lawns.

Emma said impulsively, 'What a magnificent setting!'

'My mother will enjoy showing you around,' Kane Talbot said levelly.

'*My* mother adored gardening. I remember her laughing at her grubby hands, and my father asking her why she didn't wear gloves. She said she couldn't work in gloves.'

'It doesn't sound as though she's still alive.'

Emma said slowly, 'She died when I was fifteen—almost sixteen.'

'That's a bad age to lose a mother,' he said unexpectedly.

Emma nodded. 'Yes. Too young to be able to view her with any degree of judgement—I just thought she was perfect—and I was so self-absorbed I couldn't see past my own grief. But I don't suppose there's any good age to have your mother die. Oh!'

The drive had eased around a clump of large trees and

run out in front of the homestead, a splendid, modern structure that fitted the garden and the landscape, both enhancing and being enhanced by its surroundings.

'It's lovely,' Emma breathed. 'But surely the framework of the garden is older than the house? Those trees have been here a long time.'

'The original homestead burnt to the ground about thirty years ago,' Kane said. 'After that we lived in the manager's house until my mother persuaded me to build this.'

Emma glanced up swiftly at a stony, unrevealing profile. Choosing her words, she murmured, 'It's always a shame when a piece of history goes up in smoke.'

'It happens. And this is a superbly comfortable replacement.'

Gracious, too: behind big double doors the hall opened out in tiled splendour. Lit by a wide skylight, an indoor garden planted with leafy, tropical shrubs ran in cool, soothing harmony down the entire side of the hallway, set off by the white flowers of peace lilies hovering above their glossy green leaves like small doves.

'My flight of fancy,' Mrs Talbot confided when she saw Emma's admiration. 'Kane indulges me shamelessly, even though I'm only here over summer. I'm an Australian, and winter here is too cold and wet for me, so I flee across the Tasman for nine months of the year.'

It was difficult to imagine Kane indulging anyone, but when Emma looked involuntarily upwards she surprised an ironic amusement in those enigmatic golden eyes. 'You and the architect waited until I went overseas,' he said, 'and then changed the plans.'

'It was just going to be a pool of still water,' his mother confided, 'very modern and tranquil and lovely, but I prefer plants. And—be honest now, Kane—don't you like the plants better?'

'How can I know, as I never had a chance to enjoy the water?'

His mother said sternly, 'It will be much better when

you have children. If the reflecting pool was there you'd have to put up rails, and that would spoil the look of the hall.'

A hint of reproof in her hostess's voice caught Emma's attention. She looked at Kane.

Although not a muscle moved in his face, she sensed that he wasn't pleased with his mother's comment. When he spoke it was with an inflexible undertone that made his words seem dangerously close to a warning. 'True. Shall we go through?'

As they went towards a door Emma found herself thinking that although the plants looked lovely she'd like to see a reflecting pool there, its depthless, gleaming surface emphasising the serenity of the hall.

CHAPTER THREE

THE sitting room was big, with a high ceiling and wide windows. Emma had a confused impression of comfortable sofas and chairs covered in pleasantly muted stripes, of pictures and flowers, of light gleaming on silver and mellow wood.

Waiting for them were a man, about the same age as Emma, and his sister. They made a handsome pair—he with the easy grace and good looks of an actor, she only seventeen or so, with a soft, rather petulant mouth and huge green-blue eyes.

'Rory and Annabelle Gill,' Mrs Talbot said, introducing them. 'Kane's cousins. They're spending the holidays with us.'

Rory Gill greeted Emma with every appearance of interest, but his sister had no eyes for anyone but Kane. Poor kid, Emma thought compassionately; there was a schoolgirl with a crush if ever she'd seen one!

After a perfunctory smile Annabelle emphasised, 'Very *distant* cousins! Kane, if somebody doesn't ride Asti soon she's going to be too stroppy to catch, let alone mount. I'll take her out for you if you like.'

'Thank you, but that won't be necessary,' Kane said, smiling at her. 'Emma's agreed to exercise her.'

Emma's head came up and she met tawny eyes that were cool and hard and commanding. After a prickly moment she lowered her lashes.

'Really?' Annabelle directed an accusing, chagrined glare at Emma and said sharply, 'I hope you're a decent rider. Asti's pretty toey.'

'I manage,' Emma said, noticing the tiny, hastily smoothed frown that pleated Mrs Talbot's brows.

'How on earth did you get that chance?' Annabelle demanded.

Kane said calmly, 'I offered it to her.'

And such was the power of his personality that no one said anything more about the subject, meekly following his lead as he began to talk of places that Emma might like to visit now that she was in the north.

Nevertheless, Emma was pleased when the doorbell chimed, and the neighbours, mostly considerably older than her, and friendly, began to arrive.

At dinner she sat beside Kane, and if it had been any other occasion she'd have enjoyed it very much, although she thought that the table decorations—formally arranged roses—and the silver and very expensive china were a trifle too fulsome for a dinner party in the country. Beautiful as it was, it looked like a setting from a glossy magazine.

Still, that was a personal reservation, and there could be none about the food or the company. They talked about the happenings of the district, but also of politics and national events, books and films, so that she was able to hold up her end of the conversation.

And it wasn't Annabelle Gill's narrow-eyed condemnation that ruffled her composure, either—she could deal with the Annabelles of this world. What made her uncomfortable were the times she looked up and found Kane Talbot watching her.

He didn't stare and he certainly didn't leer; no, this was a speculative, probing regard, as though she was something new to his experience. He was probably more accustomed to sophisticated women, she thought with a rare flash of self-consciousness, picturing a blonde, long-legged Australian almost-fiancée with manicured fingernails, seriously good jewellery and Versace clothes.

After the superb meal Mrs Talbot fended off compliments with a charming reference to her housekeeper's skill and hard work. Kane's mother was an excellent hostess, making sure that everyone was enjoying themselves, drawing out the shy guests, dazzling everyone with her wit and warmth.

And yet, Emma realised reluctantly, although Mrs Talbot couldn't have been nicer, whenever she spoke to her that all-embracing warmth dimmed behind a slight wariness.

Later, as they were drinking coffee in the lovely sitting room, one of the men said to Emma, 'You've got that Rottweiler of Mrs Firth's under control, I hope.'

Acutely conscious of Kane, Emma said, 'He'll be on a leash whenever I walk him, and he sleeps in the garage at night.'

'Just keep him away from my sheep,' the older man said jocularly. He meant it, however.

Hoping she could deliver on the implied promise, Emma said, 'Don't worry. He's very trainable.'

Annabelle Gill, perched on the arm of her brother's chair—to show off, Emma thought with unusual annoyance, her lovely long legs—said, 'Did you read in the paper a couple of days ago that Rottweilers are the most dangerous dogs in the country?'

'To vets,' Emma returned drily. 'Closely followed by corgis and chihuahuas. I can vouch for that—I've been severely bitten by a chihuahua that looked as though butter wouldn't melt in its tiny mouth. However, Lucky is not vicious.'

They talked dogs for a little while, and inescapably the conversation drifted to sheep-worrying. Emma listened. She knew that farmers dreaded the sporadic outbreaks of death and mutilation; she understood their concern.

One of the men remarked, 'Of course the best way to keep a dog safe around sheep is to train him as a sheepdog.' He looked across at Emma. 'Perhaps that's what you should do with the Rottweiler.'

Emma said, 'They were bred to be guard dogs. I don't think—'

'You said he was intelligent,' Kane put in casually. 'I've got a puppy I'm putting through her paces. Bring Lucky up and we'll see how he goes with sheep.'

His guests grinned and tossed the idea around, making jokes, guessing how a trainer would deal with something as naturally dominant as a Rottweiler. Emma sat silently, wondering why Kane Talbot had made the suggestion.

But it might be a good idea...

Although she could handle Lucky, she didn't know if Mrs Firth was strong enough to deal with him when he grew to maturity. Many people weren't; she'd seen enough big dogs, bred to guard, who terrorised their owners or the public because they hadn't been trained with any understanding of their natures. Eventually many followed their protective instincts to the extreme, and had to be put down after attacking an innocent bystander.

She said, 'But if he gets the idea that he's entitled to be around them, wouldn't that make him too interested in sheep?'

They considered this. The man who'd first suggested it said, 'Can't see it myself. If he's trained to work them he'll only do it on command.'

And Kane, who seemed to understand the way her thoughts were going, said coolly, 'It's worth a try. A big, intelligent dog needs work to keep active and interested. Sheepdogs have been trained to use their instincts to control sheep rather than attack them. There's no reason why a different breed shouldn't be at least taught not to chase them.'

Mrs Talbot smiled. 'Let's hope it succeeds,' she said cheerfully, and gave the conversational ball a neat little twist that spun it in a new direction.

Shortly afterwards a dismayed Emma realised that the safety pin she'd used to secure her slip strap had come undone and, apart from savagely jabbing her shoulder, had relinquished its hold on her slip.

Affronted by the prospect of revealing a scoop of satin

beneath her hem, she waited until her hostess was free and explained her predicament.

'Oh, dear, how annoying! There's a powder room along the hall,' Mrs Talbot said. 'I'll show you where it is.'

Although small, the powder room was luxuriously fitted and decorated with a throwaway charm that was informal and friendly. Family photographs hung along one wall in a kind of mural. Emma saw Kane in various stages—a child laughing at a large dog, an adolescent who'd managed to avoid the gangly stage, a young man sitting completely at ease on a horse.

Hastily she forced herself to look at the other photographs. One image—repeated several times—hit her like a kick in the stomach. Dark, brilliant eyes looked out at the world from a tense face; dark hair was dragged back in the child, drawn sleekly away from the lovely, adult face that bore a faint resemblance to Kane's.

'My stepdaughter—Kane's half-sister,' Mrs Talbot said, following Emma's gaze. 'Diane's mother died when she was very young, so when I married her father I suppose I should have expected fireworks. However, I was very young myself, and I had no idea how a child could react to a stepmother. I expected it to be roses all the way, and fortunately Diane is as sweet-tempered as she is beautiful, so she accepted me happily. When Kane was born a year later she fell in love with him—not a sign of jealousy!'

'How wonderful.' Emma knew this. She'd been told by Fran Partridge, the gardener, who was pleasantly garrulous about the neighbours. She'd revealed that Mrs Talbot had been much younger than her husband, and that the marriage had broken up when Kane was barely five. Emma strove to say something—anything—to hide her odd reaction, but her mind said *Diane, Diane,* and for an appalled moment she thought she might faint.

'She's ten years older than Kane,' Mrs Talbot said chattily, 'but they were great mates as children. I used to call

Diane his second mother. They're still very fond of each other—whenever he's in London he stays with her.'

Emma regained enough equilibrium to say woodenly, 'How nice. Thank you. I'll just hitch up my petticoat.'

Mrs Talbot was watching her in the mirror with faintly puzzled eyes. 'There's a sewing kit in the second drawer.'

Desperate to get her out of the room, Emma pinned a vague smile to her stiff lips. 'Thank you.'

When the door closed behind her Emma sank down onto the chair that stood in an alcove and closed her eyes. Oh God. Oh God oh God oh God…

But after a moment of wild panic she stood up and opened the drawer. Methodically she got out of her dress and slip, threaded a needle and stitched up the strap. It gave her something to do while she reeled at the horrible coincidence that had sent her to the house where Diane, the woman Emma's father had wanted to marry—the woman Emma had driven away—had lived.

She'd never known her as Diane Talbot. An early marriage had given her another surname—Emma couldn't remember what.

An inchoate dream died, one Emma hadn't even been aware of cherishing. There was now no chance of ever being more to Kane than a very temporary neighbour. She'd ruined any such hope seven years ago, when she'd been sixteen, grief-stricken and outraged—and determined and devious. Hindsight had a habit of exposing actions in a particularly harsh spotlight; this one couldn't be any harsher.

She wondered whether she should tell Kane, but dismissed the idea. 'Oh, by the way, I'm the woman who wrecked your half-sister's love affair seven years ago. I was only a kid, but I knew what I was doing and she knew I was doing it. Sorry about that—hope she didn't take it too hard…'

No, it was over and done with, long gone, and it didn't sound as though Diane came home from the other side of the world very often. Let sleeping dogs lie, Emma thought, neatly snipping the thread.

Anyway, she hadn't dreamed any dreams—that was ridiculous. Kane was engaged, or so close to it that it made no difference, and Emma's experience of relationships where one of the partners wasn't free had filled her with nothing but contempt for people who indulged in them. He was an attractive man, that was all, and like every other woman in his house that evening she'd responded to his disturbing masculinity. It meant nothing.

Nothing at all.

Back in the sitting room, Emma was accosted by Rory Gill, who grinned at her with appreciation as he confided, 'I'm really glad you're here. Most of Kane's neighbours seem pretty old and set in their ways. It's quite surprising, really; in Auckland he moves in *very* high circles—the highest—and in Wellington too. He's used to dealing with top people in government, and very well thought of he is, there and overseas. Somehow it always surprises me to see that he hasn't lost the common touch.'

Snob. Emma said lightly, 'Country people are conservative by nature—they have to think in terms of years and generations, not days or weeks—but most of them are intelligent and progressive.'

'Oh, they're the salt of the earth,' he conceded with a lazy smile, 'but very earnest and worthy. Not exactly scintillating conversationalists. Perhaps we can go about a bit together while we're here.'

'Are you on holiday?'

He didn't avoid her eyes, but there was something evasive about the way he said, 'Not exactly. When our parents decided to swan off on safari in Kenya, Annabelle wanted to spend her holidays here. As you may have noticed, she has a massive crush on Kane, poor kid. I have to do a bit of swot so I got study leave and came too. There's too much going on in Auckland—and I don't resist temptation well.' This last comment was said with a conspiratorial smile and a glance that was probably intended to be a compliment.

Emma ignored it to ask, 'What are you swotting for?'

'An executive MBA,' he said, 'while I work my way up from the bottom in Dad's firm.' He gave her a sideways glance, as though to make sure she realised that an executive MBA took brains and persistence.

He'd established his position in life very effectively. And no doubt working for his father made study leave simple to obtain. Some people had it easy. Nodding, Emma enquired, 'When do you finish?'

'Next year.' He smiled with the confidence of a man who knows he's very good-looking. 'And all work and no play is not good for Jack and Jill. Or Rory and Emma.'

Emma had no intention of accepting his offer, if that was what it was. He wasn't, she thought, as confident as he'd like to be; in spite of that slight air of superiority he hadn't opened himself to rejection.

Annabelle's arrival made it unnecessary for her to answer. Eyeing Emma with resentment, the younger woman said, 'You've certainly stirred things up in this neighbourhood. Let's hope your dog doesn't end up being shot.'

'He's not my dog,' Emma said evenly. 'He's the much loved pet of a woman who'd be shattered if he chased sheep.'

Annabelle shrugged. 'Not as shattered as the farmer whose sheep he worried,' she returned, her expression changing so swiftly that even if she hadn't sensed him Emma would have known that Kane was joining them.

'I was just telling Emma that dogs can do a lot of damage to stock,' Annabelle told him as she leant against him and gazed seriously up into his face. 'I'm sure she thinks we're all being a bit alarmist.'

Emma's skin prickled, as though she wore her knowledge pinned to her sleeve for him to see. Hastily she said, 'No, I've seen sheep that have been killed by dogs.'

Kane frowned. 'How did that happen?' As he spoke he moved slightly, so that Annabelle was no longer pressed against him, yet not so far that she would see it as deliberate rejection.

Well done, Emma thought, trying to reassure herself that she wasn't suffering from a nasty little pang of jealousy. How could she be jealous of a schoolgirl?

'When I was out running one morning I found about thirty sheep who'd been worried,' she said. 'I had to help the farmer shoot the ones that were too far gone, and when my boss arrived I helped him patch up those that were going to survive. I don't want to see it again.'

'You look far too young to be a vet,' Rory said, taking his time about eyeing her.

'I'm a practice nurse for a veterinary clinic.' Emma knew she sounded a little short, but she found Rory's interest false and demeaning. If he thought these people dull and provincial then that was how he saw her too, so his interest was either solely physical or a pastime to keep boredom at bay. She didn't know which was more insulting.

Annabelle shuddered. 'I couldn't do it,' she said. 'I know it's stupid of me, but I just couldn't kill anything.'

'Let's hope you never have to.' Emma kept her eyes steadfastly away from Kane's face, but she could sense his annoyance and wondered whether it was directed at her or his rather silly cousins.

'You don't sound as though it affected you at all,' Annabelle said wonderingly.

By now thoroughly irritated with both brother and sister, Emma smiled. 'I threw up afterwards, so I must have been upset. But people do what they have to—and I'm sure you would too. I think it's human nature to want to help something that's suffering unbearably.'

'Yes, of course,' Annabelle said vaguely.

Kane said, 'Emma, Mrs Blennerhasset would like to talk to you about a holiday she and her husband are planning in Taupo. Do you mind?'

'Not in the least,' she said promptly, smiling impartially at brother and sister as she left them. Halfway across the room Kane said austerely, 'If Rory becomes a nuisance, let me know.'

Emma drew in a deep breath. 'Thank you, but I'm able to look after myself.'

'They're both spoilt,' he said with a chilling detachment. 'Too much money thrown their way and not enough expected of them.'

'He says he's doing an executive MBA.'

'Supposed to be.' He sounded abrupt. 'He's intelligent enough to get there—whether he's got the stamina is another point entirely.'

Emma said gently, 'Don't worry about me, Kane. I know I look fluffy and inept, but I'm not, and although it's rather nice to have the offer of brotherly advice I really don't need it.'

They had almost reached the elderly woman sitting beside her husband on a sofa. Kane slowed, and said with a swift, savage smile that made her stomach lurch, 'Fatherly advice, I think, is more like it.' His smile altered, became transformed into pure masculine charm, and Mrs Blennerhasset's face lit up as she met its full force.

Relieved, Emma sat down with the elderly couple and listened as they told her what they'd like to do in her home town.

She stayed with them until eventually someone made a move towards the door. Once one person had checked their watch others followed, and within ten minutes the room was empty except for Emma, the Gills and the Talbots.

'How are you getting home?' Rory Gill asked her, flashing another of his practised smiles.

Without expression, Kane said, 'I'm taking her.'

Annabelle opened her mouth, then closed it again. A sensible second thought, Emma decided after a fleeting glance at Kane's harsh profile. If he wanted his distant cousin to come with him he'd ask her.

But she couldn't dismiss so easily the momentary flash of anxiety she'd seen in his mother's eyes when he spoke. Was Mrs Talbot a snob too? Or had she made the connection between Emma and the girl who'd smashed her stepdaughter's life seven years before?

It was highly unlikely. Don't get paranoid, Emma told herself sturdily. Kane's hard, dominating features only revealed what he wanted them to, and he wasn't the sort of man to parade his emotions. And his comment about fatherly advice made it quite obvious that he didn't feel anything like her helpless, stupid fascination. He was merely being his normal paternalistic self.

It had rained again, and as the car moved down the drive the headlights picked out the slender wet trunks of the magnolia trees and the huge pointed buds that glimmered a second before being extinguished by darkness. Shivering, Emma settled back into the seat.

At the bottom of the drive Kane said, 'I'll pick you up at nine tomorrow morning to go riding, and after that we'll give Lucky a workout.'

'We'll walk up,' she said firmly. 'The exercise will do Lucky good.'

'What if he creates havoc amongst the stock on the way?'

Emma said coolly, 'If it makes you feel better I'll put him on a choke chain.'

'Can you manage him on a choke chain?'

Ignoring his sceptical tone, she replied, 'I won't need to because he'll walk at heel like a gentleman.'

The car turned out of the gate and began to cross the road. 'All right,' he said, as though giving her permission.

Every hair on the back of her neck bristled. Really, the arrogant, overbearing—

The big car jerked to an abrupt, jarring halt.

'What on earth?' she gasped, hauling herself upright on the seat, the safety belt hard across her chest.

'The Rottweiler is out,' Kane snapped.

Sure enough, loping towards the car was Lucky, black and gleaming as the night.

'Put him in the back,' Kane ordered, leaning over and opening the door.

'He's wet—'

'Water I can deal with,' he said grimly. 'Blood is a different story.'

Lucky scrambled into the back of the car and obeyed Emma's curt command to sit. 'I don't know how on earth he got out,' she said unhappily. 'And he's been out for some time—he's really wet.'

'You might have left a window open.'

'No, I went around and locked them all.' She'd done that before she'd begun to get ready.

He said, 'It's simple enough to miss one.'

'I didn't miss one,' she returned hotly. 'I double-checked, as I always do, because the house isn't mine.' But the doors—had she done the doors? She'd run out of the front door when Kane came so he didn't get wet—had she forgotten to close it behind her? No, because he'd have noticed. What about the back door? Try as she might, she couldn't remember locking it.

When the car stopped at the gate she reached for the handle, but Kane said, 'I'll do it.'

He opened the gate, then without speaking drove through and took them around to the gravelled parking area at the side of the house where he turned the car to face the road.

'Stay here,' he commanded.

He got out and the security lights came on, revealing a half-open back door. Emma said, 'Oh, hell!'

Lucky whined and followed it with a short, sharp bark.

'Get over behind the wheel,' Kane Talbot said quietly, 'and lock the doors.'

'I—'

'Do it.' Before she realised what she'd done, she'd obeyed that peremptory order and was scrambling across.

Kane gave her the keys, long fingers wrapping hers

around the biggest. Speaking so softly that she could barely hear the words, he said, 'Turn the engine on.'

After a moment's fumbling she obeyed, and the motor purred into life.

'How's your night vision?'

'Excellent.'

'Then don't switch the headlights on. Drive the car past the gate and if I'm not back in five minutes—or if you see anyone else—go back home and ring Emergency.'

'But—'

'Just do as you're told. I'll take the dog.'

Clearly agreeing that this was serious male business, Lucky sprang out and began to eagerly sniff the ground; he went to heel when commanded and followed Kane into the house, leaving Emma in the locked car.

Fortunately the car was an automatic, so she didn't have much trouble easing it slowly down the drive and through the gateway. Staring with widened eyes into the night, she admitted that if there was an intruder inside she'd only be a nuisance to Kane, but it was terrifying to have to sit still and wait. For the first time Emma realised how isolated the house was; although there were neighbours within half a mile they were hidden behind hills, and there were no warm, reassuring lights.

As long as Lucky didn't bark, she thought, Kane would be all right.

A movement down the road caught her eye. Her heart thudded and the coppery taste of fear flooded her mouth until she made out the tired, limping form of the corgi.

'Oh, Babe,' she whispered, and leaned over.

She had to lift the drenched dog into the car; relocking the door, she settled her on the floor in front of the passenger's seat before she resumed her anxious peering. Apart from the familiar little noises of Babe cleaning herself up it was very quiet, although above the soft purr of the engine she could hear a morepork call from the patch of bush up on the hill across the creek.

The security light snapped off. Mrs Firth had told her it stayed on for ten minutes, so Kane must have found the switch.

She'd have to tell Mrs Firth that she'd been burgled, and that it was her fault. In spite of the warmth of the heater, the skin on her face and arms was cold. Babe snuffled and made little clicking noises with her teeth as she scoured her paws. The engine hummed.

Emma stared at the house. Kane had taken a torch with him, but there was no sign of its light through the blank black windows. Well, there wouldn't be; as well as double-checking that they were closed, she'd pulled the curtains across.

If Kane called would she hear him? The sudden cry of the morepork gave her the answer. Yes, she'd hear Kane. And she'd certainly hear Lucky.

Time stretched, looped on itself, dragged sullenly past. Emma glowered at the dashboard clock. Only three minutes! Rubbing her arms, she stared into the darkness. The trunks of the trees in the garden solidified slowly as her eyes became accustomed to the lack of light. They looked, she thought, spooky, and what could be spooky about two cabbage trees, a loquat and a jacaranda?

Nothing moved. Apart from the low murmur of the engine, there was no sound.

And then she jumped, because Kane materialised out of the night, a looming, silent figure with Lucky a blacker shadow at his heels.

Emma opened the door.

'Nobody's there,' he said, speaking with his normal crisp authority, 'and as far as I can see nothing's been disturbed. Out you get.'

Feeling absurdly self-conscious and small, she switched off the engine and scrambled out from behind the wheel, asking breathlessly, 'Was the front door locked?'

'Yes.'

'I must have forgotten to shut the back door,' she said guiltily.

'That's what it looks like,' he said, not bothering to hide the note of condemnation in his tone.

Emma said in a muted voice, 'It's the sort of thing you do so automatically that your mind doesn't register it.'

'Or forget to do and not register it.' At her shamefaced nod, he said, 'You'd better come inside and make sure nothing's been taken.'

Angry with herself, and yet relieved that she'd got off so lightly, she said, 'All right. Oh, wait a minute—I'll get Babe.'

'You let her into the car?' His voice was low and dangerous.

'Yes.'

'A stupid thing to do when for all you knew there could have been someone out there.'

She threw him a haughty look. 'The door was only open for a moment.'

'When I tell you to do something,' he said with a lethal, silky inflection that sent a swift shudder the length of her spine, 'I expect you to do it.'

Wrenching the door open, Emma scooped the wet dog up and held her against her breast like a buckler. 'I couldn't leave her out in the cold.' She stopped, concentrating fiercely on controlling the waver in her voice, then continued with as much dignity as she could muster, 'Thank you for checking out the house. Believe me, whenever I go out in the future I'll make sure I lock everything.'

'Everyone makes mistakes. Get off your high horse,' he said, cool mockery underpinning his words, 'and follow me into the house.'

Fuming, she obeyed, followed closely by Lucky. Once inside Kane switched on all the lights, including the security light again, and after snatching a towel from the laundry and wrapping the corgi in it Emma walked steadily through every room in the house, always preceded by the tall figure of the most aggressive man she'd ever met.

'Nothing's missing,' she said on a sigh when they'd arrived back in Mrs Firth's pretty sitting room. She bent and put Babe down. The little corgi sniffed about interestedly, then made for her basket by the rocking chair.

Giddy with relief and shame, Emma added, 'At least, nothing that I can see.' Keeping her eyes well away from the man in the doorway, she gazed around again. Lucky sat down and scratched himself vigorously.

'In that case,' Kane said, his voice infuriatingly unemotional, 'I think we can conclude that no one's been inside. The dogs' behaviour backs that up too. No fascinated questing after new scents. If anyone had broken in they'd have pinched alcohol and the video recorder at the very least. Would you rather stay the night at Glenalbyn?'

For a moment she wondered where he meant, until she remembered the painted sign beside the gates to his property that said 'Glenalbyn', with his name and initials beneath it. He was offering refuge.

'Oh, no,' she said, firmly ignoring the craven part of her that urged her to accept. 'Thank you, it's very kind of you, but we'll be perfectly all right.'

'In that case I'll head for home. I've checked all the windows and doors. Lock the door behind me.'

'Thank you,' she repeated with brittle composure.

'It was nothing,' he said, dismissing his part in the evening with laconic and rather insulting ease. 'Have you got my telephone number?'

Astonished, she stared at him. As her eyes were snared by the hot amber of his, awareness licked across her nerves, wakening her body but dulling her brain.

'No. Why?' she asked uncertainly.

He went across to the telephone and wrote a number down on the pad there. 'I noticed there's a phone beside the bed; if you need me, ring and I'll come down.'

'That's very kind of you,' she repeated woodenly.

'Goodnight.'

She accompanied him to the back door, locked it, and stood there as the car started up and moved quietly away from the gates.

Ears straining, she listened while he closed the gates and drove onto the road. When at last the sound of the engine had died away and the only sound was the morepork in his lonely, death-dealing vigil, she shivered.

Lucky whined at her heels, and she said, 'Although I must have left the wretched door open, I think I'll bring your beanbag in from the garage so you can sleep inside tonight. After I've dried you both down, of course.'

It took her half an hour to get them both clean and dry and settled, and herself showered and dressed for bed.

Once there she lay for a long time, listening to the soft, sweet gurgle of the stream at the bottom of the garden, the little waterfall freshened enough by the rain to splash over the rocks.

Kane had made sure she was safe in the car, then gone into the house with only a half-grown dog for protection, moving as silently, as purposefully as a hunter in the darkness. There had been something eerie about the way he'd been swallowed up by the night, as though it was his heritage.

And you, she told herself, are being absurdly fanciful, because you're ashamed and you don't want to remember that you were so aware of him you forgot not only to lock the door but to close it. When you think about him your brain goes on holiday and your body takes over, which is embarrassing and stupid and totally useless.

She'd just have to make sure that she didn't get too close to the people in Glenalbyn homestead. It shouldn't be difficult; after all, she was only going to be there for three weeks. It was a nuisance that she'd agreed to exercise the horse, but she could find some excuse for staying away, and no one—especially not Kane—need discover her connection with Diane, or learn of the pain she'd caused seven years ago.

Eventually she drifted off to sleep, waking in the morning to the sound of the telephone at the side of the bed. Fortunately she didn't suffer from early morning languor. Picking up the receiver, she said briskly, 'Hello.'

'How did you sleep?' Kane Talbot's voice was slightly rough, as though he'd only just got out of bed.

It was extremely intimate to lie there and listen to him. Emma's gaze wandered across the soft pink duvet cover; she straightened out toes that had curled.

'Fine, thank you,' she said politely. 'No problems. I let Lucky sleep inside just in case, but he didn't even bark.'

'Good.'

She set her chin and said, 'I'm not usually so unreliable.'

Amusement gave an added dimension to his tone. 'I'm sure of it. Don't worry, everyone's allowed a slip-up now and then, and the chances of any burglar coming along and finding that door were pretty remote. All's well...'

Another voice—Rory's—could be heard in the background. Kane said, 'I'll see you at nine, then. Goodbye.'

'Goodbye.'

It was nice of him to call, she thought, setting the receiver down. And he was right, although that sick feeling returned in full force whenever she thought of the door open and the two dogs roaming. However, no harm was done, and it certainly wouldn't happen again.

Because Babe was lethargic, and it was cold outside after the night's rain, Emma decided not to take her to Glenalbyn. A short walk at midday when the weather report promised sun and warming temperatures would be better for her arthritis.

After breakfast she and Lucky set off. Although she wore jeans and a serviceable jersey, an impulse she should probably have resisted had persuaded her to tie a scarf around her neck. The blue and black silk set off her grey eyes and fair skin, but when Kane came out to meet her at the homestead there was nothing more in his glance than a maddening hint of amusement, and she realised she'd worn it to look good for him.

Scolding herself for the pique that set her teeth on edge, she summoned a smile. He looked different from the man who had flowed into the night's darkness like a deeper shadow, but there was no mistaking that air of physical mastery. This was a man who rarely, if ever, came across a situation he couldn't control.

'No Babe?' he asked.

'No, she's limping this morning, so she can rest.' She paused, then ploughed on, 'I didn't thank you enough last night for making sure there was nobody in the house.'

'You thanked me quite enough,' he said, the golden eyes coolly assessing. 'Not that I need thanks—any other man would have done exactly the same.'

'Perhaps,' she said, wondering if he believed that, 'but I'm glad you were there. I'd have been frightened if I'd been alone. It would have served me right, but—'

'I hope,' he interrupted curtly, 'that if you'd driven yourself home you'd have had the sense to turn around and come straight back here.'

She was going to tell him that no, she wasn't in the habit of asking for help, but she could see it would be wasted effort. So she said, 'Well, it's immaterial now, and it won't happen again. Where's this horse?'

CHAPTER FOUR

ASTI was a bay mare, graceful and spirited, with a patrician nose, and a white star on her forehead. Like many another female she responded to Kane's unconscious, overt masculinity with flirtation, whuffling into his face, nuzzling the broad chest. He stroked her with gentle hands, talked to her in a deep voice that sent a primal shudder through Emma, and after giving the mare a carrot passed another to Emma.

'Thanks,' she said. 'There you go, pretty lady,' she murmured, holding the carrot in the palm of her flattened hand. 'Oh, you are a beautiful girl aren't you? A lovely thing...'

Her voice rippled out and over the mare, soothing, calming, soft and seductive.

Asti accepted the offering, chewing it thoroughly while Emma rubbed her forehead and patted the glossy neck, still talking evenly, mesmerically, until the mare—accustomed to Emma's scent and voice—bent her neck to examine Lucky.

The dog reciprocated with his own form of recognition and the two animals, although still watchful, came to some sort of silent understanding.

'Good boy,' Emma said. 'Sit.'

Lucky moved back and sat.

With the intriguing hint of roughness in his voice more pronounced, Kane said quietly, 'That's some bedside manner you've got. I imagine you hypnotise every animal you meet. Why aren't you doing a veterinary degree?'

She shrugged. 'The circumstances weren't right.'

'Why?'

Moving quietly, she bridled the mare, standing so that

he couldn't see her face. 'After my father died I found out that there was no money.'

'He left you penniless?'

Damn the man, couldn't he see that she didn't want to talk about this? She said quietly, 'He was a developer, and things were on a downturn. He'd have come back if he'd lived, he always did, but the house had to be sold to pay off his creditors. The furniture went for just enough to cover my fees at polytech and a year's board in Auckland.'

'Didn't it ever occur to him that you needed some sort of safeguard in case anything happened to him?'

Emma bit her lip. 'It never occurred to him that he wouldn't live for ever. He was only forty when he died.'

Kane's eloquent silence left her in no doubt about his opinion of her father's attitude.

Lightly, dismissively, she said, 'Anyway, I enjoy my life and my job, so don't go feeling sorry for me. Yearning for things you can't have is a big waste of time.'

Hitching the reins to the fence, she turned and endured Kane's hard look with equanimity, one hand stroking the mare as she recalled with ruthless clarity the caressing note in his voice when he'd talked to the animal. Was that what his voice sounded like when he was making love?

Heat collected in the pit of her stomach, honeyed and slow, leaching the strength from her bones, sharpening her senses to painful acuity. It hurt that Kane's eyes were speculative and guarded, as enigmatic as some hidden mystery of the past.

Lucky broke the taut moment with a long, elaborate yawn.

'He's obviously accustomed to horses,' Kane remarked.

'There were horses in the paddock next door to Mrs Firth's house in Taupo. He used to play with them.'

'Asti's been around dogs all her life, so if he behaves himself she'll be all right. She's sweet-tempered but she needs firm guidance,' he said. 'Think you can manage her?' Piercing eyes lanced through Emma's composure.

She said, 'I'll give it a go.'

While he bridled and saddled a large black gelding, she got the mare ready. Lucky stayed at her heels, watching with interest, only barking when she swung up onto Asti.

'Quiet,' she ordered, and he subsided. The mare danced a little, but understood after a minor battle of wills that Emma knew what she was doing, and accepted the guidance of reins and knees without any further demur.

Emma looked down at Lucky and commanded, 'Heel.'

'We'll go for a couple of hundred yards along the race with him,' Kane said, 'and then bring him back and put him in an empty dog run. If he stays at heel we'll take him out further tomorrow, and see how he goes when he's confronted by sheep in the paddocks.'

It was a good idea, and it worked. As they rode down the fenced, metalled road that led to the back of the farm Lucky stayed obediently far enough from Asti's hooves not to be in danger, close enough to maintain that psychological link between Emma and himself. He didn't much like being left in the dog run, but he accepted his fate, watching mournfully and silently as they left him.

'You were right,' Kane remarked. 'He's quick to learn.'

'Very,' Emma said, wondering whether she should be doing this. When Mrs Firth came back Lucky would find his days somewhat dull. Then she forgot about him.

She'd expected Kane to sit well on the horse—he probably did everything well, including, murmured that sly interloper in the corner of her mind, making love—but he was a world-class horseman.

Emma knew she was good, but she'd never ride like that; man and horse moved like a single entity, flowing in a harmony that spoke of skill and knowledge and a deep affection for each other.

About half a mile along the road that connected the front of the property to the back, Kane glanced down at her and asked, 'All right?'

'Fine.' After swallowing to ease a dry throat she said, 'It's a glorious morning for a ride.'

'Any morning is a glorious morning for a ride.' His voice was abstracted, making the conventional answer almost a rebuff.

'True.' Determined not to be affected by his moods, Emma looked around, breathing in the crystalline freshness of the air as she admired the smooth patina of good husbandry, of well-made fences and gates, of money spent to keep the land productive.

They'd been climbing steadily away from the homestead and suddenly the sea appeared, gleaming like a silver sheet beyond the hills to the east. Somewhere over there was the main coast road that led to Parahai and eventually to Cape Reinga, where two oceans fought for dominance around the turbulent northern tip of New Zealand.

Behind the coast, lines of hills softened by tree-filled gullies repeated the same basic shapes, row upon row advancing inland to the higher, bush-covered spine of the long Northland peninsula.

'Where are your boundaries?' she asked, because it seemed a neutral subject and she needed to break the silence.

Kane gave her a lazy, slanted smile. 'In the east we stop at the main road. We go inland as far as the forest reserve.'

Because her heart bumped at that smile, she waited a moment before saying, 'That's quite a size.' Several thousand acres at least. And, because she didn't want to sound as though she was impressed by that, she added perhaps too quickly, 'It must keep you busy.'

'I have a manager,' he said. 'I have other commitments so I can't give this place my undivided attention.'

Reins held loosely in his hand, he touched his heels to his gelding's sides. Delighted, Emma followed suit, and before long they were galloping along the wide, grassy verge of the race. Emma abandoned herself to sheer exhilaration, her hair flying from beneath her helmet as she relished the sparkling day and the high, foamy clouds, the vivid colour of the grass, the cool, fresh sweetness of the air rushing past.

When at last Kane reined in she was laughing. He looked at her with a sudden glitter in the depths of his tawny eyes, a glitter he banished immediately.

It was like a slap in her face.

'Good girl,' Emma said, making her voice warm and enthusiastic as she leaned forward to pat the mare's neck, and hid her face from the cold blaze of his scrutiny.

'You can ride,' Kane said.

She straightened. 'So can you. Have you competed?'

'Cross-country,' he returned laconically, 'before I got too big. It's best to be lean and fine-boned for a sport like that. Anyway, I didn't have time to take it any further.'

In answer to his unspoken command, the big horse turned away and settled into a canter.

Kane Talbot, Emma decided, was a very private man. Those harsh features hid his responses very well, and he kept them under strict control. What was he hiding?

Nothing. You're indulging in romantic thoughts, she scoffed, saying, 'Let's go, girl,' as she nudged the mare into following him.

A little spoilt by her easy understanding of animals and most people, she shouldn't assume when she met someone who seemed unreachable that he was deliberately blocking her. Behind that poker face, Kane was probably yearning for the woman in Australia.

At the top of a hill they dismounted and tethered both horses on the fence, then walked across to the edge of a steep face and looked out over valley and river and hills painted all the greens there could be, from the fresh spring ardour of the grass to the sombre blue-green shadow of the high trees on the escarpment across the valley, where the silver glint of a waterfall scattered between trees like a diamond necklace on a rich tapestry.

Taking in a lungful of air, Emma said, 'What does it feel like to own so much beauty?'

He looked at her, his mouth sternly austere. 'Land doesn't belong to anyone. It's held in trust for the future.'

Emma nodded slowly. 'I suppose it is,' she said thoughtfully.

His children, he meant. And grandchildren. Almost certainly he was dynastic by nature and breeding. Kane didn't view his inheritance as the money it represented—which Rory would—or even with simple possessiveness. There was an equivocal note in his voice when he spoke of it, as though it meant much more to him than he was prepared to admit. Emma hoped the almost-fiancée wanted a family.

He said nothing more, and although Emma would have liked to initiate some pleasant social chitchat—somehow this silence made the moment too significant—she couldn't for the life of her come up with a subject that wouldn't sound contrived.

Acutely aware of him beside her, she looked out over Kane's land. And because something stirred and flexed inside her, something she'd never experienced before, she was careful not to turn her head.

Instead she concentrated on their shadows stretching out before them. Beside his tall, commanding one, hers looked short and dumpy, the hard outline of her helmet a definite, rather comic finial. Kane wore an Akubra, low-brimmed, everlasting, the Australian countryman's iconic hat.

Emma was not overweight, but because her own features and limbs were softly rounded she'd never look like Annabelle Gill, with her long, long legs and angular cheekbones. For just one moment she found herself envious of the younger woman.

Only for a moment—until common sense returned, and with it a searing flash of shame. She wasn't competing with a teenager for Kane's attention! Even if Annabelle had been six years older Emma wouldn't compete—the idea made her hot with pride.

Apart from the fact that he wasn't free, he was Diane's half-brother, and the last words Diane had ever said to her were, 'Some day, you little bitch, I hope you realise—by suffering it yourself—just how much misery you've caused.'

Kane's magnetism wasn't personal; it wasn't directed specifically at her. It was just the sort of man he was.

Pointing down into the valley, she asked, 'Is that the little river that flows into the sea at Parahai?'

'A tributary. It joins the river just above the bridge on the main road.' He smiled. 'I used to swim in those pools—see, down there towards the clump of totara trees—when I was a kid.'

'But not now?'

He shrugged. His profile was chiselled out of angles and planes, the square chin and hard jawline and straight nose forming a strong framework that would last all his life.

'We have a pool at the homestead, but I don't have time to use it much,' he said after a few seconds. 'Perhaps that should be I don't *make* time. And, talking of time, we'd better get back.'

It was another rebuff, but Emma nodded. 'Yes.'

Half an hour later she stood with Kane and the newly released Lucky at the wooden rail of the horse paddock, watching the mare pace across the grass before stopping beside a brown and white goat and lowering her head to conduct a whickered conversation.

'Fergus,' Kane explained. 'He's lived in the horse paddock for ten years now. He seems to keep them quiet. Or perhaps he's just an excellent confidant.'

A swift, accusing voice from behind said, 'Oh, there you are! I thought you'd gone into the village, Kane.'

They turned to see Annabelle, very suitably attired in jeans and a jersey and boots, her auburn hair catching the sun's light and reflecting it with a shimmer of pure red. She gave Emma a smile with no warmth. 'Hello, Emma. Did you have a nice ride?'

To Emma's outraged astonishment Lucky made a little rush towards her, barking.

'No!' Both Emma and Kane shouted the word.

Shamefaced, the dog skulked back to take up his position at Emma's heels. 'Stay,' she ordered.

'He's dangerous,' Annabelle said loudly, her white face revealing how afraid she was.

'I'm sorry he frightened you,' Emma said. 'He's not dangerous, and he knows he shouldn't have rushed out like that. He wouldn't have hurt you. Truly, he's not ever bitten anyone. I don't know why he did that, but I promise you he won't do it again. Hold out your hand and let him sniff the back of it, then he'll know you're a friend.'

Annabelle didn't move; with quivering chin and shaking hands, she fixed her great eyes on Emma. 'That's easy for you to say,' she blurted. 'What would have happened if you hadn't been here?'

'*He* wouldn't have been here,' Emma said, sorry for her. 'It's all right. I'll put him on a leash.'

Lucky knew he'd behaved badly. As Emma slipped the clip onto the ring in his collar he gave her a swift, apologetic lick.

Straightening up, she said, 'There, he's safe. Won't you let him get your scent?'

She knew Kane was watching her, knew that he'd have noticed the resemblance to the tone she'd used when she was gentling the horse, but he said nothing.

Annabelle shivered. 'No, just keep him out of my way. I was attacked by a dog once,' she said curtly.

It would be useless to try and convince her that Rottweilers didn't go around seeking and destroying all living things. Emma knew that the trauma of such incidents needed skilled help.

'I'm sorry,' she said with compassion. 'That must have been terrifying, but Lucky is usually very even-tempered. He won't try it again.'

'I'll take your word for it.' Keeping well away from the

dog, Annabelle made her way to Kane's side. 'I came out to tell you there's a call from America that your mother said you've been waiting for. They're ringing back in half an hour.'

Frowning, he said to Emma, 'If this is what I think it is, I'll be busy for the rest of the day.'

'Yes, of course.' Emma was only too glad to get out of there. 'I have to get back, anyway. We've been away for longer than I thought we would be, and Babe will be wondering where we are. And I'm expecting a phone call too.'

'Who's Babe?' Annabelle asked. After Emma's explanation she laughed with a touch of malice. 'You really *are* a nursemaid,' she said. 'Nanny to a couple of dogs!'

In Kane's mouth those words had been amusing, although it hurt that he'd repeated them to this girl. 'That's it,' Emma returned cheerfully, although her smile made her teeth ache as she added politely, 'Thank you for the ride, Kane. Asti is lovely.'

'My pleasure,' Kane said with a cool, unsettling look. 'I'll take you home in the Land Rover.' Without waiting for an answer, he nodded to Annabelle. 'Would you mind telling my mother I'll be back in five minutes?'

She flashed a resentful glance at Emma, but said, 'All right,' and left them, hips swaying in what she no doubt hoped was a seductive motion.

Unfortunately Kane wasn't watching. 'Wait here,' he told Emma, and strode off towards the large implement shed that formed part of the complex of buildings and stockyards near by.

He couldn't have been more abrupt if she'd been a dog he was training. Emma's black brows met across her nose, and her lashes drooped in a look that would have warned her father and friends. She did not like being ordered about by anyone, much less an autocratic man with more personality than she had sense.

Perhaps, she thought with exasperation, that's how people behave when they get to Kane's age without anyone ever saying no to them.

She should have said she'd walk home; she'd only accepted his offer of a ride because of the call she was expecting from Auckland friends who'd left a message on the answering machine a couple of days previously to tell her they'd be in the area soon. She didn't want to miss their call, and, although she was almost sure she'd set the answering machine before she'd left, she couldn't remember doing it.

Frowning, she stroked Lucky's sun-warmed head. It wasn't fair to blame Kane for her unusual scattiness; she had to stop behaving like a halfwit.

Lucky stiffened, then leapt to his feet and turned. He didn't growl, but his ears flattened slightly. Not Annabelle again, surely! Emma thought as she turned to see who was coming.

No, Annabelle's brother, tall and amazingly handsome, his teeth flashing whitely as he laughed and called, 'I come in peace!' from a safe distance.

'Heel!' Emma commanded, wondering why Lucky mistrusted these two. Normally he enjoyed meeting new people.

She waited until he was sitting, then said, 'He's all right. Don't worry.'

'I'm glad you've got him on a leash. Blood will out, they say, and Rotties aren't exactly noted for their loving kindness.'

Exasperated, Emma still managed to smile. 'If they were as fierce as people say they are,' she said evenly, 'they'd have been extinct centuries ago. People don't keep dangerous animals around unless they can control them.'

'I suppose you do it by rewarding them with food,' he said.

Emma laughed. 'Oh, Lucky's definitely a slave to his stomach,' she said lightly, 'but he makes friends easily.'

'Will he make friends with me?'

'Yes, of course.' The sound of the Land Rover cut off her offer; they both looked up as the vehicle drew to a stop beside them. Kane pushed open the door and said curtly, 'Hurry up, Emma.'

She said goodbye to Rory and climbed in, settled Lucky at her feet, and only then gave Kane a smile of scintillating sweetness.

His brows drew together. Putting the vehicle in gear, he said levelly, 'What's the matter?'

'Nothing,' she said without emotion.

He directed a sardonic glance at her. 'All right, so I didn't wait for an answer. Most women grow out of sulking by the time they reach twenty.'

'I,' she said evenly, 'am not sulking.'

One corner of that hard mouth tucked up into what was almost certainly a smile. 'Could have fooled me. I expect Annabelle to pout, but you have a lot more presence than most women of twenty-three.'

'Probably because both my parents had died by the time I was eighteen,' she retorted, then wished the words unsaid.

'I suppose that's it.' Silence as they travelled down beneath the pink and white glory of the magnolias, their scent blowing in through the windows in great, intoxicating gusts. 'It must have been shattering for you,' he surprised her by saying.

'I managed.'

To her complete and utter astonishment he dropped a lean, callused hand over hers and squeezed, before removing it back to the wheel.

'It takes guts and stamina to deal with body-blows like that,' he said.

Emma stared at the tanned length of his fingers, the long palm, the sinewy wrist. Everything about him was oversized, but his hands were not clumsy. And they could be amazingly gentle.

They could also send a shock wave of excitement thundering through her. She glowered down at her own hands, folded primly in her lap, the short nails pink against the faded blue of her jeans, the fingers curved almost innocently.

She'd been attracted to men before, enjoyed their kisses, even accepted some mild caresses, but until Kane Talbot touched her she'd never felt lightning strike in the pit of her stomach and run through to her womb in a spasm of savage sensation.

She didn't like it. Or rather, she liked it too much.

This man was Diane's half-brother, and if not exactly engaged he was in some sort of committed relationship. He'd touched her because he was sorry for her, not because he wanted to feel her skin against his.

Thank heavens the Land Rover was turning into the gateway. 'I'll get out here,' she said quickly. 'Thanks for giving us a ride back. It was a super morning. Thank you.'

All right, so she was gibbering, but that and letting Lucky out got her over those febrile moments until her body calmed down.

'I'll see you tomorrow,' Kane said, obviously not affected by anything like her incandescent response to him.

Avoiding a direct answer, she slammed the door and waved. 'Goodbye,' she called as the vehicle backed efficiently out of the gateway.

After the Land Rover had left Emma collected the mail and the newspaper from the letterbox on the side of the road, then opened the gate and walked up the drive, with Lucky eagerly sniffing his way along the ground behind her as though he'd been away for months instead of a couple of hours.

'I know how you feel,' she told him on an exhaled breath as she unlocked the back door and stooped to pat Babe, patently glad to see them.

Five minutes after she'd checked the answering machine—grateful to see that she *had* set it—her friends rang up and organised lunch with her the next day.

When she put the receiver down Emma filled the kettle

and switched it on, trying to forget those moments when Kane Talbot had wrapped his hand around hers. She'd felt both threatened and protected, comforted and terrified, and she was still suffering the aftermath of that explosive surge of sensation.

'Physical attraction,' she told both dogs as she made herself a cup of tea. 'You know all about that, don't you? Although I suppose you don't.' Babe had been spayed when she was a few months old, and so far Lucky hadn't shown any signs of interest in the opposite sex, although it wouldn't be long.

Darn it, she wasn't some high school girl at the mercy of her first experience of lust. All right, so she was still a virgin, but that didn't mean she hadn't been tempted, although now she couldn't recall the faces of those boys and men she'd thought so attractive. Her virginity was a choice; she'd seen a friend's brother die of Aids and she'd decided that she'd never make love without protection.

Then she'd read somewhere that condoms failed ten per cent of the time and concluded that it would be much less nerve-racking to simply say no until she met someone she could trust, someone she loved enough to make that final step into commitment.

Nevertheless, she hadn't lived in a convent.

Which made her violent response to Kane's touch so surprising. She'd been so determined to see Kane as the dominant male she'd almost managed to ignore the sexuality that smouldered beneath his controlled façade. Of course the two went together: the leading male in any mammal group mated with the females and fathered the children.

Uncomfortably hot, Emma finished the tea, shut Lucky into the garage and got out the vacuum cleaner. Lucky hated it, and barked so loudly and defiantly that he was always banished when it came to cleaning time.

She should, she thought grimly, searching out the burgeoning troops of daddy-long-legs that had responded to spring's seduction by hatching out families of tiny, frail replicas, do something that gave her no time to think of the way Kane had looked on that black gelding.

Unfortunately, murdering baby spiders didn't exactly provide her mind with diversion. Nevertheless she stuck at it, until she came to the bathroom. For a moment she stood in the door, frowning slightly, her eyes ranging around the small room.

A bunch of freesias perfumed the air with their citrus scent. She'd picked them the day she arrived and they needed tidying up—the first flower on each head had died. Her comb and brush, deodorant, the lipgloss she'd put on this morning...

Everything was just as it should be, and yet she had the uneasy feeling that something had changed.

'Oh, don't be an idiot,' she said aloud. 'You're getting paranoid.'

That episode with the door last night really was getting to her. Instead of accepting the blame she was being self-serving and cowardly, trying to convince herself that it hadn't been her mistake.

Muttering, she diligently finished vacuuming every room in the house, then dusted. After that, accompanied by the dogs, she went out into the garden and weeded a wide bed of overgrown ranunculi underneath the sitting-room window, insensibly taking comfort from the classical form and vivid colours of the flowers.

Because Mrs Firth had been in the house for such a short time before the summons from her daughter had dragged her across the Pacific, she hadn't yet brought the garden into submission; she had plans, she'd told Emma, and Fran Partridge was going to be a great help when it came to putting them into action. So far she'd organised a small vegetable garden to one side of the drive behind the feijoa hedge; a chook pen was next on the list.

The sun had warmed the still air to a pleasant laziness. The very first monarch butterfly flapped elegantly over a border, this way and that, seeming to consider each flower.

Eyes gleaming with covetous interest, Lucky got to his feet and started towards it.

'Don't even think about it,' Emma told him, and he subsided, but kept a close watch on the bright orange and black wings.

The sound of a car coming slowly down the drive opposite set Emma's heart skipping. 'I'm not going to turn around,' she told the dogs, both of whom had pricked up their ears.

She didn't, but it took a real effort of will. Well before it stopped in the gateway, however, she knew it wasn't Kane.

Getting to her feet, she saw a very smart sports car with Rory Gill climbing out. 'Hi,' he called over the dogs' clamour. 'Is it safe to enter?'

'Wait a minute.' She called the dogs to order and made them both sit before she said, 'Come on in.'

'I can see why you'd want that big dude to obey you,' he said as he walked across the lawn, 'but the little one should be let off basic training, surely?'

'Lucky will let me take his biscuits away from him. The little one,' Emma told him, smiling, 'won't let anyone near her food. If you get between her and her bowl Babe goes for the bone. Your bones.'

He eyed the corgi with such comical alarm that Emma burst out laughing. 'I know corgis snap,' he said, 'and you said something at dinner about them being just as dangerous as Rottweilers and chihuahuas, but I didn't realise they were lethal. Is the Rottie a softie?'

'Well, I wouldn't say that.' Emma dropped a handful of weeds into the barrow. 'He's probably more dangerous because he's not trained properly; he might not always answer a command.'

'Would he defend you if someone attacked you?'

She looked down at Lucky. 'I think he would. He's accepted me as leader of his pack, and when Kane pulled up behind us a couple of days ago he positioned himself between Kane and me and was obviously ready to do his duty.'

Rory said, 'I'd better make friends with him, then. How do I do that? Somehow the usual friendly preliminaries you go through with the neighbourhood Labrador don't seem to be quite enough.'

'Oh, you'll be all right,' she said drily. 'Hold out your hand and let him smell it. Lucky, friend!'

Lucky got to his feet and sniffed the outstretched fingers, then relaxed, although he stayed aloof. Babe pushed her way past, and Rory went through the same procedure. The corgi's stump of a tail wagged. Babe was the reason Mrs Firth had decided that no other dog of hers should be docked.

'Right,' Rory said, obviously pleased, 'so now I'm accepted. I wondered if you'd like to come into Parahai. I have some shopping to do and we could have a cup of coffee, perhaps go for a walk along the bay.'

Mrs Firth's car might be ready. Emma said, 'Yes, if you'll wait a few minutes while I clean up.'

'I'll just sit in the sun with the dogs,' he said, and settled onto a seat beneath a flowering cherry tree, lifting his good-looking face to the sky.

After Emma had scrubbed her hands and face and changed her clothes she rang the garage and was told the car would be ready in a couple of hours. If Rory wanted to come home earlier she'd stay in the village until it was ready, which would save her the ten-minute drive to take the mechanic back after he'd returned the Volvo.

Clad in narrow black jeans with a short-waisted, slim-fitting knit top in the same soft grey as her eyes, she went out and called the dogs.

'That was quick,' Rory said, getting to his feet. 'Annabelle takes about three hours to get ready for school.'

Ignoring the lingering appraisal in his eyes, Emma said briskly, 'Oh, you grow out of that as you get older,' and shut the dogs inside. After checking that both front and back doors were locked, as well as the windows, and that the answering machine was set, she rejoined Rory.

'Did you have a good ride this morning?' he asked as they got into the car.

'It was great. Asti's a lovely mare.'

He grinned lopsidedly. 'And Kane rides like a god, so Annie says.'

'I've never actually thought of gods riding horses, but he's got an excellent seat and hands.'

'I know,' he said, skidding slightly as he went too fast into a corner and got tangled up in the drift of gravel on the side of the road. 'Whoops, sorry about that. Annie's been moaning all morning because she gave up Pony Club for ballet when she was ten, but she's with Kane now, visiting friends in Whangaroa, so she'll be happy.'

Rory was entertaining in a light-hearted way. In Parahai he bought a car magazine and posted two letters, so Emma deduced that his business in the village had been merely an excuse to ask her out. She refused to examine the fact that she was amused rather than flattered by this.

After that they went to the coffee bar where she'd been the day she'd brought the car in to the garage, and drank coffee and talked while the fountain chirruped above its fringe of pansies.

Rory was shallow and very young compared to his cousin. Although he tried to hide it, he had a pretty good opinion of himself.

When they'd emerged into the main street Emma said, 'I'm picking up Mrs Firth's car on the way home, so if you'll just drop me off at the garage—or here, and I can walk down.'

He pulled a face. 'No, I'll drop you off at the garage.'

But first they went down to the wharf, where they looked over several yachts, and while Emma dreamed of roaming the South Pacific Rory told her of much bigger ones owned by his father and his friends.

'I've got a speedboat,' he said offhandedly. 'Sailing's all right, but I like something a little faster.'

A lot faster, Emma agreed silently, judging by his car.

Several hardy high school children arrived and began to dive into the estuary, yelling encouragement to each other. Was that how Kane had been—sleek and tanned and exuberant—when he'd swum in the river pool?

Even as something clenched in the depths of her stomach Emma knew that he'd never been as noisy. He was too self-contained. Was it a hard school that had taught him such mastery of his emotions? His mother obviously loved him, so had his father been too grim, too much of a disciplinarian to give his son unconditional love?

She'd never know, Emma thought with sudden desolation.

'That's an odd expression,' Rory teased, leaning closer to gaze into her eyes.

'I'm just enjoying the sun,' she murmured, closing her lashes against the shimmer of its rays across the water.

Not too much later she collected the car and drove in front of Rory all the way home, pulling into the gateway as Kane's big car came down his drive.

Both she and Rory got out. 'The cavalry, do you think?' Rory asked.

'Who needs rescuing?'

He laughed, and she laughed with him, but her whole attention was bent on the car that swung towards them and came to a halt just behind Rory's.

Even before Kane got out she knew he was in a black rage. Nothing showed on his face—the tough features were clamped in a mask of control—but an icy, dangerous fire burned in his eyes. Involuntarily Emma braced herself.

Rory turned, his smile still on his face, and said, 'Yo, cousin.'

'Sorry to disturb your afternoon,' Kane said, his voice even and as piercing as a knife. That frozen gaze hadn't left Emma's face. He continued, 'I've just heard that two dogs savaged a flock last night—they killed three lambs, and three more had to be put down. Luckily the owner heard the noise and got out before they killed the rest of the flock. He didn't get a good look at the dogs, but he said there was one large one and one small.'

CHAPTER FIVE

EMMA had been afraid a few times in her life—when she'd realised her mother was going to die, and when her father had brought Diane home and told her they were getting married. But she'd never been afraid of a person.

She was now. Adrenalin pumped through her, tightening every muscle in a primitive fight-or-flee response. Before she could say anything, Kane looked at Rory and said, 'I'd like to speak to Emma alone.'

Rory started. He'd been looking at his cousin with something like the fascinated horror a snake feels when confronted by a mongoose. Taking a step backwards, he babbled, 'Oh, OK, yes, fine, see you later, Emma,' and got into his car, backed out of the driveway and sped off with more than the usual sputter of gravel.

Craven, although she didn't blame him.

Emma took a deep, painful breath. 'Where did this happen?'

'About four kilometres away.'

Relief flooded through her as she shook her head. 'Then it can't have been Babe and Lucky—Babe can barely walk one kilometre, let alone four.'

His glance cut through her like a polar wind. 'You have no idea how far she can go,' he said in a voice that ripped her excuse to shreds. 'Just because Mrs Firth thinks she's too old to walk more than a few hundred metres doesn't mean she can't. And with your job you should know that.'

He was right, of course, but she protested, 'She's also arthritic. And you were here last night—you saw both dogs. Neither of them had blood on them.'

'They had to cross two creeks to get back here, so that would have washed any blood away. Did you check?'

'I dried them both down; there was nothing except mud on the towels.' She didn't try to hide the stiff note of anger in her voice because it concealed her growing dread and guilt.

He said brutally, 'Because you were careless—'

'You don't have to tell me,' she interrupted, cheeks scarlet. 'All I can say is that it will never happen again.'

'See that it damned well doesn't.'

He turned and got into his vehicle. After watching him back out and take off down the road, Emma climbed back into Mrs Firth's car and drove up and into the garage.

Inside she scrutinised the two dogs, both delighted to see her, neither looking at all like sheep killers, and felt sick.

'Oh, hell,' she said shakily. 'What have I done?'

Her carelessness in leaving the back door open could have signed their death warrant. Once dogs developed the taste they went back time and time again, until they were either shot in the act or put down.

Looking at Babe spread out gratefully in the sunlight pouring through the window, Emma said desperately, 'There's no way you could struggle several kilometres over hills and creeks!'

And although both *had* been soaked to the skin, it had been raining last night. However, Kane was right. She couldn't swear that it hadn't been Babe and Lucky, and so she owed the farmer the money those dead sheep were worth.

Without anything more than a panicky hope that her bank balance would stand it, she rang Kane's number. His mother answered, and although she enquired after Emma's wellbeing her voice was cool, and turned cooler when Emma asked to speak to Kane.

Emma looked at her white knuckles, consciously relaxing her fingers while she waited.

'Yes?' His voice was deep and hard and unyielding.

'Who was the farmer whose sheep were killed?'

'Why?'

Anger lit a small, sullen ember inside her. She said, 'Because I need to know.'

'Why?'

Emma said, 'I should recompense him for the dead ones.'

He hesitated a nano-second, then said curtly, 'There's no need for that. It's not proven; he wouldn't take your money.'

'Even so, I want to know who it is,' she stated, holding onto her temper with an effort she hoped didn't show in her tone.

'I'll tell you when he's had time to simmer down.' Another silence, one she refused to break. He said, 'Just make sure those dogs don't get another chance.'

Emma had never been worried by a volatile temper—most of the time she considered herself to be rather placid. It was one of the reasons that she was so good with animals; they responded well to her calmness. However, at that moment she could quite easily have given in to a massive tantrum. 'They won't,' she said grittily. 'Thank you. Goodbye.'

She replaced the receiver with exaggerated care, realising with an odd sort of detachment that her hand was trembling.

Kane Talbot was an arrogant, overbearing, arbitrary, *rude* gorilla. Although he had every reason to be infuriated by her carelessness, he had no right to withhold the name of the aggrieved farmer. That was between her and the farmer, and Kane had nothing to do with it.

Clearly he was royally furious with her. Good, because she was furious with him. If she never saw him again that would be too soon. His girlfriend was welcome to him.

Because her touring friends, Selena and Brian, rang early in the morning to suggest a picnic, Emma saw him in less than twenty-four hours.

Fell over him, actually. It was raining again—one of

those sudden, extreme thunderstorms that pounce out of a blue spring sky—and as she'd forgotten her umbrella she dashed across the supermarket car park and into the foyer, stopping abruptly to avoid a trolley.

Knocked off balance, she took two wavering steps sideways and cannoned into a solid body. Ruthless hands came out of nowhere, burning through the thin, wet material of her shirt, and she looked up into eyes the cold yellow-brown of a lion's. Her treacherous body sprang to life.

'I'm all right,' she said automatically, the words jouncing around like the fat raindrops splattering on the asphalt outside.

Kane held her until she got her balance, then let her go as though she'd seared his fingers. 'You're wet.'

'I'll dry.' She was going to wear those fingermarks for a long time. Her heart gyrated in her chest, robbing her brain of much-needed oxygen so that she couldn't think logically.

However, a primitive instinct of self-defence warned her that instead of standing there staring at him like an idiot she'd better get out of his orbit and into the safety of the supermarket aisles.

Giving him a curt, dismissive nod, she turned away and headed for the inner door. Once inside she let out her breath in a whoosh, only to have her heart lurch when she realised that he'd followed her.

'Yes?' she asked, looking just past him.

His eyes glinted. 'I'm not going to apologise for what I said yesterday.'

Emma summoned a jaunty smile. 'I didn't expect you to,' she said dulcetly, not unpleased with the way his brows drew together slightly.

He looked formidable. 'Or the way I said it.'

She was still breathless, but at least her brain was working once more. Widening her eyes, she let her lashes droop. 'I didn't expect *that*, either.'

Of course he knew what she was doing. That glint in his eyes turned into a predatory glitter. 'I'd like to talk to you.'

'Sorry,' she said smoothly, 'but I've got both dogs in the car so I can't spend too much time in here. Besides, I'm going on a picnic with friends and I want to make a pie before they come to pick me up. Special request—Brian adores bacon and egg pie. Another time, perhaps.'

Giving a smile that hovered perilously close to the borders of smugness, she nodded and turned away.

'Most of the beaches around here,' he said coolly, 'are banned to dogs at this time of the year because the shore birds are nesting. And dogs are forbidden on all of the reserves all of the time.'

'I'm leaving them at home,' she said abruptly, and marched down between the bread and the soft drinks.

As she swung into the next aisle she allowed herself a little peep over her shoulder. No sign of a tall, big man with black hair and the cold eyes of a predator.

Which was just as well, she told herself, half-appalled at her behaviour. Talk about twisting the tail of the tiger!

Still, if he thought she could be so easily charmed into overlooking his arrogance of the day before, it was time he learned she wasn't a push-over. Other women might hang breathlessly on his every word, but Emma had a little more pride.

She snatched up a packet of bacon, angry because she'd been so intent on getting away from Kane that she'd forgotten to pick up a basket, let alone a trolley. Juggling the bacon and a wedge each of Brie and New Zealand blue cheese, she scooped up a packet of already rolled short pastry, tomatoes and a roll of salami and headed for the express checkout, hoping she could balance them all until she got there.

Kane turned her brain to cottage cheese.

No, that was unfair; he didn't do it deliberately. Whenever she saw him logic got swamped in a heady mix of emotions and a physical response that sent her blood surging, and jittered across every nerve-end. And that, however reluctant she was to admit it, was an indication of desire, and she'd felt it from the moment she set eyes on Kane.

Well, she could just stop it. Leaving aside—as if she could!—the fact that he was almost engaged, Emma didn't believe in love at first sight, and attraction was common coin; she'd get over it. When she left Parahai she'd never see him again.

And if nothing else could tame the wild, sultry urgency that scorched through her at the sight of him, there was Diane. It was all very well to say that what had happened seven years ago shouldn't matter now, but an event like that cast a long shadow down the years. Kane loved his half-sister; he wasn't going to look kindly at a woman who'd caused her such pain.

Not that Emma cared what he thought.

He wasn't anywhere in the car park when she emerged. With disappointed relief she endured the noisy welcome of the dogs, put the groceries into the boot and drove sedately home over wet roads, not even looking at the Glenalbyn driveway.

Lucky suddenly barked in her ear. 'Stop that,' she commanded, then fell silent as she too saw the dark green car parked on her drive.

Ruthlessly squashing white-hot anticipation, Emma drove through the open gates and stopped, keeping her eyes averted from Kane's lean form lounging against the side of his car.

He straightened up and came across, opening her door. As the dogs scrambled to get out Emma shouted 'Sit!' in her most ferocious voice, and, given their confined quarters, both dogs did the best they could.

'You'd make a good sergeant-major,' Kane commented, his voice amused.

'Perhaps I should take it up,' she said, turning away to open the back door. 'Out,' she said, noting that Lucky waited to let Babe go first.

So Babe was still the dominant member of their small pack. She probably would be until she died. And when that happened Mrs Firth would find out whether she'd managed to convince Lucky that he was where he should be, and very definitely a subordinate.

Back straight, head held high, Emma went to the boot and opened it.

'I'll carry that,' Kane said, and a long arm scooped up the paper bag.

Frustrated, because she couldn't think of a polite way to keep him out of the house, she called the dogs to heel, stalked beside him to the back door and unlocked it.

In the kitchen he deposited the groceries on the bench and watched while she put them away. Emma's mouth tightened, but she switched on the oven and got out the rolling pin and pie dish and donned an apron.

'You look very domesticated,' he said. Mockery gleamed in the amber depths of his eyes, wound through his words like cream stirred into coffee.

Damn it, he thought she was funny. Two more weeks, she told herself, that's all.

And ignored the sharp, stabbing prick of desolation.

'Most women are,' she said, baring her teeth slightly. 'It's a matter of having to be. Men still renege when it comes to housework.'

'I know,' he said, and watched as she unwrapped the pastry. He met her disbelieving look with a shrug. 'I make my bed and can cook a meal of sorts. My father believed that every man should be able to look after himself.'

Not his mother. No, Emma thought, lining the pie dish with quick, deft movements, Mrs Talbot would have indulged Kane to the limit.

She arranged the bacon on the pastry and broke the eggs, sliding them carefully onto the bacon so that they didn't break.

Kane said drily, 'Asti missed you this morning.'

Emma reached for parsley from the bunch on the

windowsill and began to chop it. 'I left a message on your answering machine.'

'I got it. A very precise, clipped voice, clear and exact. You were very sorry but you wouldn't be able to ride.' He watched as she mixed the bright green parsley with cream and added nutmeg and salt and pepper. 'Was it because I snarled at you yesterday?'

Carefully, Emma poured the speckled cream over the eggs and bacon, and covered the pie with the remaining pastry, turning the dish in her hand as she cut off the surplus. 'We didn't exactly part on good terms.' She put the dish down and began to make leaf shapes from the leftover pastry.

To her astonishment, he picked up the utensils she'd used and stacked them into the sink.

Although she kept her gaze on the small pastry decorations, from the corner of her eyes she noticed his hands, the competence of his lean fingers. He didn't waste effort; his gait, his stance, the way he walked, were smooth and pared down of all superfluous movement. And he moved with such fluid economy that it became grace, a masculine emphasis of the virile magnetism of his height and body.

'I was angry,' he said with no apparent concern, 'but it's over. I don't hold grudges.'

The oven pinged, indicating that the right heat had been reached. Emma opened the door and slid the pie in. 'That's very worthy of you,' she said as she closed the door and stood up, thinking wistfully that perhaps she didn't need to worry so much about Diane.

His eyes narrowed. 'You clearly do.'

'Hold grudges? I hope not—anyway, I felt too sick about the sheep to resent your attitude. But I did object when you decided that you wouldn't tell me who the owner of those sheep was.' Her voice teetered on the edge of stridency. Reining in her temper, she finished, 'I'm not used to other people making decisions for me, and I don't like it.'

He was watching her from half-closed eyes, his heavy-lidded gaze sending shivery little pulses through her body. Thoroughly ruffled, Emma glowered at him.

'If you see him now,' he said calmly, 'he'll probably say things that will not only upset you but will make him feel ashamed when he's had time to get over it.'

'In other words,' she said pleasantly, 'it's still no.'

His mouth tightened. 'If that's the way you want to see it.'

'It's the only way to see it.'

He said, 'It's obvious that you're an only child, the focal point of your parents' existence.'

Emma bared her teeth. 'How astute. I imagine the same could be said of you.'

'Having an older sister made all the difference,' he told her, his eyes gleaming ironically beneath his dark lashes. 'You learn tolerance and give and take when you have siblings.'

Emma bit back the words that trembled on her tongue. Quarrelling with him wasn't going to achieve anything. If she'd been intending to live there for any length of time she'd fight harder for her independence, but she'd be gone very soon. Until then she could suffer his autocratic behaviour.

'Tolerance and give and take? Really?' she asked, in the tone of a woman making polite chitchat.

His mouth twitched. 'So people say.'

'How nice for you.' And let him think what he wanted to of that!

Infuriatingly, the twitch turned into a full-blown smile that smashed straight through her defences and demolished them. Desperate, Emma cast about for some other topic of conversation.

He provided it for her. 'So I'll see you tomorrow morning,' he said.

Emma's shoulders moved slightly, but she said, 'Yes, all right.'

'And make sure you bring that dog. I'll start him off with my pup.'

Startled, Emma met the full blazing impact of those tawny eyes. 'Why?' she demanded. 'Surely now he should be kept away from sheep.'

'He'll learn that he never goes near them unless he's been given a direct order. That's why sheepdogs don't chase sheep.'

It made sense.

'And you'd better stay,' he finished with cool decisiveness, 'so that you can see what I'm trying to do. It may well be the one thing that will stop him from being shot one day.'

Reluctantly Emma nodded. Lucky combined determination and persistence with intelligence and the ability to learn fast. He needed the discipline of excellent training, and a lot of exercise as well.

'Will you keep doing it when Mrs Firth comes back?' she asked.

His expression hardened. 'Yes,' he said uncompromisingly.

Whether the older woman wanted him to or not, Emma deduced, taking refuge in irony.

Oh, well, by then she'd be in Hamilton, out of reach of Kane's forceful magnetism.

'Which should make you feel better when you leave here,' he added.

'Yes.'

He saw too much, understood her too well, and she didn't like it because he kept his innermost thoughts and responses hidden, presenting to the world only the controlled, inflexible armour of his self-possession and his authority.

That decisive control reduced Mrs Firth's charmingly decorated kitchen to a frame for his formidable male presence. 'If it's not too early, I'll see you tomorrow at half past seven.'

'I'll look forward to it,' Emma returned with a hint of sarcasm. Unfortunately that was exactly what she would do, and it worried her.

Still, he couldn't make much of a dent in her heart in the time she had left at Parahai—not if she was sensible and refused to give that unruly organ any licence to falter.

When he'd gone she let the dogs out of the garage and threw a ball for them both until Babe gave up and stretched out, panting, in the shade of the flowering cherry tree. Then Emma exhausted Lucky with a fast, hard game.

Eventually she picked up the tired corgi and carried her in, listening to Babe's rapid breathing, watching the stiffness with which she settled into her basket. As Emma took the gleaming golden pie from the oven she was convinced that Babe couldn't possibly have gone through the creek and over the hills at the back of the house; she'd have been too exhausted to get back.

So there had to be another two dogs that were worrying sheep, and for Lucky and Babe's sake she hoped they'd be caught soon. Frowning, she packed the rest of the food into the chilly bin and got ready for the picnic.

Selena and Brian arrived dead on time, cheerful and noisy and interested in everything. After they'd seen around the garden they left the dogs asleep in the house and headed for a nearby beach. As it was a crisp day they found a spot sheltered from the brisk wind by a large pohutukawa tree, and caught up with news while they ate.

'I wish you could stay,' Emma said, draining her coffee cup.

Selena cast her husband a significant look. 'So do I, but Brian's organised this reunion with an old schoolfriend in Whangarei tonight.'

Brian, almost asleep, opened one eye. 'It's the only night he could make it,' he said peaceably. 'Sorry, Emma.'

Emma grinned. 'So am I. Never mind, you can come and stay with me in Hamilton.'

Her friend gazed curiously at her. 'That was a quick decision,' she said. 'I thought you were settled in Taupo for the rest of your life. You love the place, and you love your job, and yet between one letter and the next you'd left your job and got a new one in Hamilton! If it had been any other woman I'd have thought you'd had a bust-up with a boy-friend, but you'd have told me if you'd been serious about anyone. You'd better have!'

Emma grinned. 'I heard about the Hamilton job from a friend I met at polytech. The clinic deals with thorough-breds from the surrounding studs, and I want the chance to work with them.'

'Good career move,' Brian said sleepily.

'Then why aren't you there now, ministering to sleek, flighty, expensive stallions and mares?' Selena asked.

'My replacement at Taupo started straight away so I wasn't needed there, but at the Hamilton clinic the woman whose job I'm taking isn't leaving until the end of this month. And the unit I've rented in Hamilton has ten-ants who have another fortnight to go. So when Mrs Firth rang in a panic because Pippa wanted her to fly to Vancouver—well, my gear was already in store in Hamilton, and all I had to do was fly up here.'

'And how is Pippa?'

Emma told her, and then, while Brian gave up any pre-tence at wakefulness and slept, they drifted into reminis-cences of school days and old friends, until at last Selena shook her husband awake and said, 'If we're going to see any of the local sights we'd better get moving.'

They had a great afternoon, and when she waved them goodbye Emma was surprised by a sharp pang of home-sickness. It was, she decided, a good sign. It meant that although Kane had certainly blotted out her common sense, he probably wouldn't have any lasting effect.

'Dinner time,' she said to a prancing Lucky. He got up and followed her into the kitchen, tail wagging as she took the home-made dog biscuits from the fridge.

However, when she went to let him out for his final run

around the garden, she discovered he'd only eaten three of them.

'Are you all right?' she asked him, going down on one knee to check him out. He didn't have a Labrador's amazing capacity for food, but he normally ate everything she put in front of him.

He grinned at her, and let her poke and prod him.

'Yes, you're all right,' she said, and stood up. 'Perhaps you've stopped growing temporarily.'

She removed the biscuits and the next morning checked him carefully again, but he was clearly both hungry and in the best of rude good health.

After breakfast she and the dog set out for Glenalbyn, leaving Babe snoozing in her favourite patch of sun in the sitting room. Clad in jeans and boots, and with a sweatshirt over her cotton shirt, Emma strode through the sweet, cool air, telling herself that the excitement licking through her veins was a simple response to the glorious morning.

It had very little to do with Kane. Oh, she was attracted to him, but it was one of those ephemeral reactions, that of a nubile woman for the alpha male. Her mouth twisted wryly.

Lucky began to bark, jerking her away from her self-serving thoughts. Down the drive came Rory's red car; he stopped and the window slid silently down as he said, 'Hi, you look good enough to eat.'

'Thank you,' she said.

'He's not going to jump up and scratch the door, is he?'

'No.' To make sure, she commanded, 'Sit,' and watched with pride as Lucky did just that. He was obeying her orders with much more alacrity than when she'd first come.

'So you're going riding,' he said, taking his sunglasses off and eyeing her.

'First we ride, then Kane will put Lucky through his paces as a sheepdog.'

'That,' Rory said, his grin widening, 'is something I'll have to see. I'll be back in an hour or so.'

Emma stepped back and waved, and he drove off, too fast as usual. Summoning Lucky to heel, she walked quickly up the hill, trying to burn off her anticipation.

It didn't work. She arrived at the door of the homestead panting slightly and hot-cheeked, but with the excitement as potent as ever.

Mrs Talbot opened the door; when she saw Emma her smile faltered before returning to its original welcome so swiftly that Emma wondered whether she'd seen aright.

'Come on in,' the older woman said, holding the door open. 'Kane's on the phone, poor darling, trying to get some sense out of a man in Wyoming. He won't be long.'

'I'll tie Lucky up,' Emma said, producing the leash from her pocket. She looped one end around a post and clipped it onto his collar.

'He certainly looks tough,' Mrs Talbot said.

'He's like a loving but stroppy child,' Emma told her, removing her boots. 'He needs discipline and affection and a stable home life.'

Mrs Talbot laughed. 'Annabelle is right,' she said, urging Emma into the house. 'You sound just like a nanny.'

Emma's smile was a little stiff, but she said lightly enough, 'That's what I am at present.'

Through a closed door she could hear Kane's voice—commanding, focused—the words indistinguishable but the deep tone sending little shocks through her. He didn't sound impatient, just determined.

What would it be like to have that determination concentrated on her?

Too much, common sense replied promptly. He'd overpower you with the force of his personality—you'd be fighting to keep some part of your mind for yourself.

Mrs Talbot led the way into a room—much less formal than the rooms Emma had been entertained in on that first night, but just as pleasant and comfortable. A table set for breakfast stood in a sunny window and the perfume of freesias floated on the air, vying with a few lingering scents of bacon and coffee and buttered toast.

There was no sign of Annabelle.

'Would you like something to drink?' Mrs Talbot asked. 'Tea or coffee?'

Emma opened her mouth to accept when Kane walked through the door, clad in hip-hugging trousers and a polo shirt that clung lovingly to his wide shoulders.

'Ready?' he asked Emma, his angular features expressionless.

'Yes.'

He bent and kissed his mother's cheek. 'We'll be back in an hour.'

She smiled, her eyes going from his face to Emma's and back again. Emma could have sworn she saw something like pain in the dark depths, but if she did it was gone immediately.

Nevertheless the hint of hidden undercurrents bothered her, causing an uneasiness that wasn't dissipated by Asti's flirtatious greeting. This time Kane decided that Lucky, having proved that he'd respond to Emma's commands, should come with them. The dog seemed to realise that he was under close scrutiny from both Kane and Emma, and padded along with aplomb, keeping just far enough away from the mare's heels to be safe.

No sheep dotted the paddocks beside the race, but there were cattle. Some young ones with more energy than sense blundered up to the fence when they saw the dog, and followed him along the length of it, but although Lucky's ears twitched he ignored them.

'So far so good,' Kane said curtly, looking down at him. 'He's certainly trying to please.'

'He's a good dog, aren't you, Lucky—a good, clever dog,' Emma called out.

The dog gave her a laughing grin, his tail wagging enthusiastically.

They went through a gate; bending forward to pat Asti's

neck, Emma watched Kane latch it behind them. His hat was low on his forehead and he looked big and completely at home.

Greedily Emma noted the flexion of muscles beneath his shirt, the smooth deftness with which he managed the gate, the easy masculine grace, an amalgam of power and strength and perfect balance.

He looked up and caught her watching him. Embarrassed, she turned her head, but she'd seen swift fire kindle in his eyes.

Without really knowing why, she blurted, 'Who does Asti belong to?'

'She's mine,' he said shortly. 'A high school girl usually exercises her, but she's away in New Caledonia on a school trip.'

Emma nodded, wondering who the mare had been bought for. The almost-fiancée? 'The high school student has good hands,' she said. 'Asti's mouth's like silk; she's obviously never had anyone sawing on the reins.'

'No,' he said, and set the gelding into a canter.

Emma followed, and within a very short time both horses were galloping. Emma gave the mare her head, her whole being caught up in the thud of hooves on the damp ground, the scent of crushed grass and the mastery of Kane's riding—so effortless it looked as though rider and mount were linked by some mythical tie.

Exhilaration coursed through her and set fire to her blood. Several times she whipped her head around to see what Lucky was doing, but he never strayed from his self-appointed position.

As they approached a patch of bush she eased the mare into a canter, holding her steady when she tossed her head and tried to veer from the fence. Lucky caught them up, tongue lolling, flanks heaving, his pleasure almost palpable. Bending, Kane opened a gate onto a bush-lined track.

It was very still, the air saturated with a primeval, earthy perfume that added to Emma's internal turmoil. When Kane had asked her whether she could ride—had it only been five days ago? It seemed for ever—she should have said no.

Then she wouldn't have had to endure this silent purgatory. She was so acutely aware of him she needed all her will-power just to focus on the horse beneath her and the steep track between the trees. As well, she had to monitor Lucky. Fortunately he was still on his best behaviour, although she noticed his head swinging from side to side as he sought the origins of a multitude of new and fascinating odours.

Eventually they reached the bottom of the gully and stopped by a stream, dismounting to let the horses drink a little. Lucky lapped at the water, then began to follow a particularly interesting scent, nose down between the dark trunks of the trees.

'Here,' Emma ordered.

Unwillingly he obeyed. Frowning, she said, 'I suppose there are kiwis here. Dogs love kiwis.'

Kane said something under his breath she was glad she didn't hear.

She said hastily, 'I'll walk him out on the leash.'

'I could put him up with me.' He sounded coldly remote.

In a tight voice Emma returned, 'Your horse might not mind, but I think Lucky would.'

'I suppose so. All right.'

While she clipped the leash onto the dog Kane flipped the reins over both horses' heads, and together they walked them up the other side of the gully, beneath trees so old they were almost covered in spiky clumps of epiphytes and orchids.

'I should have realised there were kiwis here,' Emma said after several taut minutes.

'I knew.' His voice was curt, almost gravelly. 'I wasn't thinking.'

Was he so ruled by a need to control everything in his life that even a minor thing like this could send him into a temper? No, she thought after a fleeting glance at his face. That was a kind of illness, and Kane was very sane.

And he didn't seem to be angry. He'd withdrawn; she could feel a wall between them, a barrier that came from him, because she was still quivering inside with an intense absorption. She looked away, seeing his booted feet come down on the track, noiselessly as a panther. His long legs moved with a relaxed, tireless rhythm, eating up the ground so that she and Lucky had to hurry to keep up with him.

Perhaps she was becoming obsessed with him.

Well, she thought wearily, almost certainly she wouldn't be the first woman to lose her head over him.

Or the last.

But it wasn't any use pining for him, or exciting herself with the fantasies that clogged her brain—or even learning to like him. They had no future, not even as friends. He was engaged, and he was Diane's half-brother.

CHAPTER SIX

AT THE gate on the other side of the patch of bush Emma released Lucky and swung up into the saddle.

Silently they rode home again. It was a silence that endured when they unsaddled and turned the horses free, apart from a few necessary words. Lucky noticed; alert, wary, he stuck close to Emma.

Perhaps Kane was just temperamental, she thought, walking back beside him towards the homestead. However, it didn't seem likely that he'd let his moods rule him. Surely he would, as she did, consider that a weakness.

Where the drive forked she said, 'Thanks for the ride. It was glorious.' Banal words, spoken in a strained voice.

Glancing at his watch, he said, 'I have to make a phone call in five minutes. After that we'll put Lucky through his paces.'

Emma did not want to go back to the homestead with him, to be watched by his mother and the belligerent Annabelle. She said lightly, 'Would it be too rude if I stayed by the pool? I feel grubby and horsy.'

'That's fine,' he said, no emotion at all in his voice. 'I should be back in a quarter of an hour.'

Beside the pond was a seat under a spreading ornamental elm, its still bare branches sheened with a haze of gold, forerunner to the butter-yellow leaves.

Without looking at Kane as he walked on up the drive, Emma sat down, stroking Lucky's head when he pressed against her knee. After a moment he went and drank from the water, before coming back and stretching out at her feet.

Filtered sunlight spattered Emma's upturned face. She

tried to empty her mind, but Kane's image lodged in her brain, violently outlined and three-dimensional.

With weighted eyelids and a soft sensuous curve to her mouth, she remembered the easy grace with which he'd hefted the saddle onto his horse, the proudly poised head, the masculine symmetry of shoulders tapering to lean hips, the coiled strength, the angular, forceful features—and the slow, cold burn of his eyes.

But it was his mouth—that controlled mouth with its sensuous lower lip—that sent sultry little shivers through her. And the white flash of Kane's smile, compelling and masterful.

'Emma.'

Her lashes jerked upwards. He'd come so silently that she hadn't heard anything. And Lucky hadn't moved.

Because her knees were wobbly and her senses rioting, she took the hand Kane held out. He pulled her up, but when she expected him to let go he continued that deliberate, inexorable pull right into his arms.

'I've been fighting this ever since I saw you,' he said, his voice deep and low and intense, and then he kissed her, almost as though this was something he was doing against his better judgement.

It was like being taken over, swamped by such potent physical carnality that she lost contact with the rational part of her brain. There were no compromises with this kiss; she felt the hidden, secret pathways in her body soften and heat as every receptor registered the steely vitality of the man who held her.

His heart thudded irregularly—or was it simply that their two hearts combined in one driving, erratic beat? Emma's fingers spread wide as her hands pressed against his broad back. She drowned in his taste—dangerous, infinitely disturbing, magnetically male—and her bones melted in a consuming, elemental hunger.

Until sluggishly, urged by some whisper of misgiving,

she lifted heavy, reluctant eyelids to meet the narrowed, blazing glitter of his.

Thick dark lashes hid almost all of the amber depths, but the fire there was as cold as the sun's rays imprisoned in the heart of an iceberg, she thought, so dazed with pleasure, with excitement, that her brain stumbled lethargically over the jumbled images.

Cold and remote...

Pain slashed through her, mercilessly stripping away veils of delusion. Blinking fiercely, Emma stiffened and pulled away.

When he let her go she stepped back and took a shuddering breath. 'This is not a good idea,' she managed to say, despairing at the guttural note in her voice.

'No,' he returned, so distant that she flinched. 'I'm sorry.'

Lucky whined and pushed his head against her leg; she stroked around his ears, unable to fix on any of the thoughts that chased themselves through her brain. She could only feel a vast disillusion, because uppermost in her mind was the woman in Australia, the one he was supposed to be engaged to.

Still in that flat tone, Kane said, 'It won't happen again. We'd better get going.'

The next quarter of an hour was purgatory. Emma sat on a gate while Kane, with the help of two older dogs, put a sweet little black and white border collie bitch and a puzzled but intrigued Lucky through their paces.

Kane didn't seem in the least affected, whereas she was so shattered she had to summon every scrap of inner fortitude to veneer over her turbulent emotions, to accept that for him such kisses were apparently of no particular importance.

Fortunately, after a few minutes his skill at working the dogs caught her attention, and her intent concentration calmed her. He was good. Patient, with an enormous understanding of the canine mind, he rarely scolded, relying more on rewards to teach the dogs that one whistle went with one particular command. Emma felt an odd sort of pride as it became obvious that Lucky, although he had no idea of what was going on, never had to be told the same thing twice.

The hot spring sun coaxed amber and old gold from Kane's dark hair, emphasising the harsh warrior's features as, hands on lean hips, he kept an unfaltering eye on the dogs. Unwillingly Emma remembered how that wide back had felt beneath the palms of her hands, the hard hunger of his mouth against hers.

And don't forget, she reminded herself, that he was appalled at that kiss. He hated himself for doing it—and so he should.

'*Fas*cinating, isn't it?' a light voice said from behind her.

Emma turned. 'Oh, hello, Annabelle.'

Kane's cousin stood at the other end of the gate, her lovely face cool although her eyes were defiant. Avoiding Emma's gaze, she drawled, 'Kane knows where he's going. In fact my mother, who's a third cousin once removed, or something, and has known him all his life, says that he's been like that since he was a baby. He makes plans, he waits, he works; he doesn't care who he hurts and nobody ever gets the better of him.'

'Is that all it takes?'

'What?'

'I'd have thought,' Emma said judicially, 'that along with ruthlessness and determination he'd need intelligence and energy and courage. Stupid people can work hard and accomplish things, but to *always* get what you want you need brains and guts as well.'

'You've obviously been studying him,' Annabelle said with a small, feline smile.

Emma shrugged. 'I hardly know him.'

'You probably wouldn't get far even if you did. Jennifer says he's got the most infuriating habit of burying his feelings so that it's impossible to tell what he's thinking.'

So her name was Jennifer. 'I wonder why?' Emma said, keeping her eyes on Lucky, who was loping across the ground towards Kane.

'Oh, he's always been like that, but you'd think he'd loosen up a bit with the woman he's engaged to, wouldn't you?'

Emma realised that she'd been wilfully fooling herself about the state of her emotions; she still didn't know what she felt for Kane, but it was far more intense and shocking than mere physical attraction. Quick panic flared through her as she understood for the first time just how close she'd wandered to the edge, what desperate danger she'd walked into because she'd refused to examine her response to him.

'Didn't you know about Jennifer?' Annabelle asked, carefully banishing any satisfaction from her tone. It was wasted effort because her body language gave her away and her eyes were alight with a kind of desperate malice.

'We don't discuss personal things,' Emma evaded. Although the words had sounded a bit rough, she thought she'd managed to leash the desolation that vibrated through every cell.

'Perhaps you should have before you kissed him down by the pond,' Annabelle retorted, unable to control herself any longer. She ploughed a shaking hand through her hair in a gesture that pulled the heavy tresses back from her flushed, angry face. 'Her father's John Hutter, the Australian industrialist, and she's been hostess to royalty and heads of state. She buys her clothes in France and Italy and she's very charming. And she's going to marry Kane.'

Her voice was a heartbreaking mixture of misery and gloating. As though she couldn't trust herself to say any more, she turned and ran back across the paddock.

Emma dropped to the ground, but halted when Kane called her name. 'I'll take my dogs to the kennels,' he said. 'Wait there.'

Lucky came bounding up and stopped at her feet, gazing up into her face; unable to trust her voice enough to shower him with the praise he deserved, Emma stroked the black ears and shoulders as Kane strode off towards the line of kennels by the big implement shed.

Consciously controlling her breathing, trying to lose herself in the even flow of it in and out of her lungs, she fought back the dark desolation that crouched, gibbering, in the pit of her mind. Sheer will-power held her together, but when Kane returned she kept her eyes averted.

'I'll drive you down in the Land Rover,' Kane said. 'Lucky's had a fairly exhausting morning.'

Emma closed her mouth firmly over a biting refusal. The last thing she wanted to do was share a vehicle with him, but she'd go back with him this once. Because it would be the last time. From now on she wouldn't ride with him or drive with him. He was engaged and she was too close to falling in love with him.

After a silent journey he stopped at the gate. A battered old station wagon was parked in front of Mrs Firth's house with an equally time-ravaged bicycle leaning against it. As Kane's car drew to a halt a figure rose from a flowerbed and waved a pair of secateurs, and around the corner came another, shambling a little behind the wheelbarrow.

Kane leaned over and opened Emma's door. 'Fran's brought Davy with her today. Have you met him?'

'Yes, they brought some eggs in for Mrs Firth the day I came. He's a nice kid. And I see him riding his bike up and down the road.' Eager to escape, she scrambled onto the drive.

Kane got out too, followed on command by an enthusiastic Lucky, who raced towards the gardener's son. Babe came panting around the corner, and as Davy gave a whoop of delight and dropped the wheelbarrow Kane demanded sharply, 'How did she get out?'

'Ms Partridge has a key,' Emma said in her coldest voice.

He nodded, his hard eyes fixed on the laughing boy, tangled with Lucky on the grass.

Davy's mother came across, her thin, tanned face

pleased. 'Hello, Emma, Kane,' she said. 'You've been working in the garden, Emma.'

'Did I pull something precious out?'

Fran had an infectious chuckle. 'No, you can tell the difference between plants and weeds. Not many of your age can do that.'

It was said without innuendo, but after Kane's comment on her domesticity the previous day Emma felt like a prim, old-fashioned freak. Stifling her instinctive and entirely baseless irritation, she said, 'Probably more than you'd guess.'

Fran laughed. 'You're right. I shouldn't make blanket judgements about the younger generation—it sounds as though I'm sinking into middle age,' she said cheerfully. 'And we're not, are we, Kane?' It wasn't a question—more a statement of fact, made with the comfortable knowledge that he wouldn't disagree.

With a sardonic smile he replied, 'Sometimes I feel as old as Methuselah.'

After a startled moment Fran said robustly, 'Well, I never do, and I'm two years older than you.' She looked curiously from Emma's face to Kane's, and then turned to call to her son, who was rolling around on the grass with the excited dogs. 'Davy! You told me you wanted to say something to Kane.'

Reluctantly he got to his feet, dusting the grass clippings off himself. Followed by the dogs, he came over to Kane and grabbed his hand.

'Hello,' he said, enunciating carefully.

'Davy,' his mother said, 'you've got dirty hands.'

'It's all right,' Kane said, smiling at him. 'Your hands always get dirty when you're working hard, don't they, Davy?'

'Yes,' Davy said, and beamed.

Emma's heart contracted. They looked odd, the big, straight man, with everything the world could give him, and the boy of twelve or so, who showed in both behaviour and features that he'd never reach mental adulthood.

Fran prompted, 'Davy wants to thank you for something, don't you, Davy?'

He nodded. 'For the trip,' he said, and grinned at Kane. 'The school trip.'

'Did you have a good time?'

Davy dropped Kane's hand and swung his arms around. 'The mountain blew up!' he shouted.

Fran grinned. 'The school group just happened to be on Ruapehu when it blew,' she said. 'We had the most spectacular view—tell Emma and Kane what you saw, Davy.'

His eyes widened. He gave Emma a bashful smile and said, 'Fire, and smoke, and big, big clouds, and it made the snow all dirty. And it was loud. But it was a long, long way away.'

'So you had a really good time,' Kane said, his smile almost gentle, for once free of the authority Emma had thought inbred.

This Kane was new to her; although nothing would ever subdue his autocratic attitude, it was tempered when he spoke to Davy.

That the boy hero-worshipped him was obvious; within a very few minutes it was clear that Fran did too. He stayed a short while, talking easily to both, before saying goodbye and leaving them.

Aching with a foolish sorrow, Emma pushed the memory of his kiss to the back of her mind and helped them in the garden, finding some sort of solace in Davy's chatter as he wheeled the clippings and weeds away and played with the dogs.

'He loves dogs,' his mother confided, expertly shearing a hebe bush. 'He's always on at me to get one, but they cost.'

Snip-snip went the hedge-clippers. Stooping, she collected an armful of deadheads and dumped them in the wheelbarrow. 'Kane's wonderful,' she went on. 'He sponsored the whole special class—eight kids—on the trip. He heard we were having difficulty getting the money, and after we'd had three sausage sizzles he strolled into the principal's office one day and paid over enough to get us there.'

'Nice of him,' Emma said, as matter-of-factly as she could.

'He's a good man. Tough—he doesn't help anyone who's not prepared to help themselves, which is why he waited until we'd done everything we could—but he's very generous.'

And so, thought Emma austerely, he should be. He was rich.

'Without any fanfare, either,' Fran added. 'Occasionally you hear of something he's done for someone, but he doesn't like being talked about so no one knows just how much he gives.'

From a note in her voice, and her swift glance at Davy's bike, Emma deduced that he'd helped the gardener with more than just the trip. 'I suppose he feels some obligation to the place where he was born and brought up,' Emma said.

Fran shrugged. 'Actually, he was born in a very expensive nursing home in Sydney. His mother didn't want to have her baby here. And if she'd had her way he'd have grown up in Australia too, but Kane's father got custody after a really messy battle and after that Kane only saw her in the holidays. And when he went to boarding school it was only every other holiday.'

'Oh, poor little boy!' Emma was horrified. 'I thought in those days mothers always got custody of their children.'

Fran's face closed up as she bent to yank out a large sowthistle. Straightening, she said, 'It was a knock-down, drag-out fight, and in the end they settled out of court.'

'Why?'

'I don't know,' Fran admitted after a moment's hesitation. 'But it broke her heart. She hated living in Parahai, but no one could say she wasn't a good mother—not just to Kane either. His half-sister Diane really blossomed while she was here.'

Emma despised gossips; she tried very hard not to indulge. Nevertheless she said, 'It's a wonder Mrs Talbot can bear to come back.'

'She doesn't spend all of her time here—just a few months now and then—but when Mr Talbot died ten years ago, she was across here like a shot. She talked Kane into building a new house—he and his father and Diane lived in the manager's house after the original homestead burned down.'

Fran's face softened as she glanced across at her son, happily playing with the dogs again. 'Kane's parents probably shouldn't have got married—he was much older than her. She was beautiful and bright and bubbly and charming, and he was—well, dour, I suppose. My mother used to say their marriage was a nine-day wonder.'

Emma turned to look at the pink and white glory of the magnolia avenue. So much beauty, ending in such a commonplace tragedy. Behind her Fran went on, 'Kane's sister had it tough, too. I suppose Mr Talbot loved his kids, but he was one of the old school. He didn't hit them and he wasn't unkind, but he had high standards and he made it obvious he wasn't pleased when they didn't live up to them.'

Emma said carefully, 'It sounds like a bleak childhood.'

'By my standards it was. I know Diane loved boarding school, but Kane hated it. Sending him away was like caging a lion. He was always a controlled kid, but while he was away he really learned how to keep a lid on his feelings.'

So part of that infuriating control was due to his childhood. No doubt his mother had spoiled him rotten when he'd spent the holidays with her, then he'd had to come back to a father who sounded like some Victorian despot.

'Old Mr Talbot,' Fran said, leaning back to survey a bush

with narrowed eyes, 'didn't know how to deal with kids. He was old-fashioned—when Diane left school he thought she should come home and keep house for him! No wonder she married the first personable man that came along. It was a disaster, of course. Children marrying children almost always is. Then she met another man, but they broke up and Diane just about died.'

Transfixed by horror, Emma said lamely, 'How awful.'

'Well, yes, it was.' The hedge-clippers clicked briskly as the next hebe received a close haircut. 'Apparently it was the old story—he promised her he'd marry her when he divorced his wife, but his wife died first and then he turned Diane down.'

Emma opened her mouth, then closed it, feeling sick. Was that what Kane believed?

'Since then she's been single, although of course she might live with someone in London,' Fran went on. 'Mrs Talbot never remarried either.'

Not for lack of suitors, Emma guessed, wrestling with a particularly defiant dandelion. She shoved her trowel into the ground and worked around the thick taproot, determined not to let it beat her.

'I wonder why?' she said.

Shrugging, Fran said, 'Perhaps she likes the freedom. Davy, stop playing with Lucky now and empty the wheelbarrow.'

Davy disentangled himself and came across, giving Emma his charming shy smile before saying, 'Rory likes Lucky too.'

His mother looked startled. 'Who's Rory?'

'He's my friend,' Davy said. 'He's staying with Kane.'

When Fran still looked blank, Emma explained.

'Oh, yes, I know.' Fran nodded. 'He used to come up for the holidays occasionally when his parents dumped him and that pretty sister of his on the Talbots.' She looked fondly at her son, who grinned back, picked up the handles of the wheelbarrow and trundled it off to the compost heap at the back of the house.

Fran asked, 'Have you heard from Mrs Firth?'

'Yes.' Emma frowned.

'Bad news?'

Emma said slowly, 'Well, she's a little worried about her daughter. Apparently things are not going the way they should.'

'That's tough. She'll want to stay on in Canada, then.'

'She didn't say anything.' Emma didn't want to join in conjecture about Mrs Firth's possible plans—possibly to be relayed by Fran around the district—so she steered the conversation in a different direction, feeling hypocritical because she'd listened so eagerly to Fran's gossip about the Talbots.

That evening, both dogs sleeping soundly in front of the fire, Emma switched the light off and sat watching the eerie dance of the flames, finally allowing her mind to roam back to that kiss. All the emotion hadn't just been on her side. Kane had wanted her—and despised himself for it!

The knot of tension that had taken up residence in Emma's stomach gripped even tighter. She was, she admitted with profound reluctance, furious with him, and fiercely, bitterly jealous.

Like poor Annabelle.

Biting her lip, she got up to put another log on the fire. Although the evenings were warming up, her desire for consolation and reassurance had persuaded her to chop kindling and set it going.

Back in her chair, she stared into the red-gold heart of the flames, almost hypnotised by the leaping, flickering light, frowning as she tried to make sense of that embrace.

Kane had kissed her as though he was starving, as though she was the gold at the end of his personal rainbow. His desperate, driven intensity had smashed through her caution and her carefulness.

Or are you fooling yourself? she wondered cynically, trying hard to be sensible. Perhaps he's just a brilliant kisser. Perhaps that's how he kisses every woman—including the one he's engaged to.

Did he make a habit of it, following each kiss with the same abrupt, angry apology?

'And you're just as bad,' she said out loud, wincing at the rancour in her voice. 'You knew about his Jennifer, and you didn't try to stop him. You went under without a thought for her.'

Lucky got to his feet and came over, resting his head on her arm to gaze at her with dark, worried eyes.

'Yes, you know I'm feeling wretched,' she said softly, stroking around the black ears. 'It would be a lot easier if we humans could somehow sense what others were thinking instead of relying on words and actions.'

A mordant smile hurt her mouth, because right from the start some primitive female intuition had discerned Kane's interest, and understood it, and responded to that raw, male appreciation. He'd been unfaithful to Jennifer, but she was just as bad.

'Or did he kiss me on a whim,' she asked Lucky, 'because I was available and he was a man—and then feel rather stupid about it because it meant nothing to him and he could see that it really did mean something to me?'

Too much. It had meant too much. Instinct warned her that it would be best to pretend it had not been so important, but she couldn't dismiss it so easily. It had been her first real experience of passion.

With Diane's half-brother. An engaged man! No doubt the old, malicious gods were smiling at that.

Babe yawned, then sat up, suddenly alert. As though she'd given him a signal, Lucky too swivelled his head and looked towards the window. Neither dog, however, barked.

'A hedgehog, no doubt,' Emma said with wry amusement, 'and, of course, infinitely more important than my angst!'

And because she wasn't going to sit there and agonise

over an unfaithful man, she went into the kitchen to make some hot chocolate, guided by the warm light of the fire.

Soon it would be daylight saving time, and the evenings would draw out towards summer. Soon she'd be in her new unit in Hamilton; although small, and one in a row of twelve such units, it was an improvement on the cramped flat she'd rented in Taupo. For one thing, it had a garden.

It hurt, but it had to be faced. When she left here she'd go for good. Parahai was a holiday, a time out of time.

It would be different if there was any prospect of Kane loving her.

The thought slid into her consciousness so seductively that she wasn't even aware of slipping into a daydream, where Kane's hard face was gentled into tenderness and he whispered that he loved her, wanted her…

'No,' she said sharply, banishing the cloying miasma. 'No and no and no, damn it!'

Because he couldn't love her, just as she didn't love him. She'd known him for barely a week—and you couldn't fall in love in a week. Oh, she wanted him. A feverish female intuition whispered that they'd be good in bed together. But Kane was a sophisticated man of the world, older than her, wielding lightly the power that money and status give their possessors.

Even if he hadn't been engaged to another woman, Kane would never want *pretty*, ordinary Emma Saunders, who hadn't made love to anyone, who was a small-town woman with a small-town upbringing, small-town ambitions and a small-town outlook.

She'd leave Parahai, and eventually Kane's face would fade from her mind and she'd forget the kiss and the hot, erotic flavour of his masculinity. Some day she'd forget his name, the way the sun conjured flames from his hair, and the stark, abrupt angles and planes of his warrior's face—that harsh testimony to his character—would fade and die.

'Of course it will,' she said sturdily, knowing she lied, dimly aware of the sound of silent tears in her heart.

She put the milk onto the bench and got down a mug, then jumped as both dogs suddenly raced towards the back door, barking.

Emma froze. 'Who's there?' she called sharply.

No one answered, and when she pushed the barking dogs aside to test the door she found it locked. However, the harsh glow of the security light now shone through the glass pane at the top of the door. Emma stood tensely with a hand pressed to her surging heart.

It wasn't always prowlers that triggered security lights. Almost certainly the dogs' reaction had been a response to a wandering dog—perhaps, she thought, the ones that had killed the sheep. Or a hedgehog. Even a scuttling rat could trigger them.

Whatever, it had gone, because the dogs returned to lie in front of the fire without any further signs of interest.

Normally the night held no terrors for Emma, but she found herself shaking slightly as she sat down in front of the fire with the mug of chocolate, and that night she let Lucky stay on his beanbag in the sitting room.

Neither dog stirred while Emma lay wooing sleep for hours. When at last unconsciousness claimed her it brought dreams—vivid, bewildering fragments of desolation and loss, of panic and confusion, that left her unrefreshed and aching with misery.

A misery that lasted in a muted form for the next two lonely days.

At seven the following morning the housekeeper from Glenalbyn rang to tell her that Kane wouldn't be able to ride with her for some days as he was going away.

He couldn't have made his rejection more plain. Emma set her jaw and went on with life, because although she missed him fiercely she wasn't going to let herself admit it.

On the third day she woke to rain and a warm, wet wind—a storm blowing in from the north with enough turbulence to indicate its tropical origin—and a telephone call from Mrs Firth, who said almost without preliminary, 'My dear, Pippa is finding this pregnancy very difficult and wants me to come and live here.'

'I'm sorry,' Emma said gently. 'What can I do?'

On what sounded suspiciously like a sob, Mrs Firth said, 'If I do decide to stay here I'll get my solicitor to arrange the sale of the house, but I'll have to trespass on your good nature by asking you to organise the dogs. I don't know whether they'll need to be quarantined or for how long. Could you find out?'

'Yes, of course—'

'Emma, what can I do about Babe? If we have to quarantine her she'll almost certainly die. Last time she was in kennels she didn't eat—'

'Don't worry,' Emma interrupted. 'Would it make you happier if she lived with me instead of emigrating to Canada? She and I get on really well together, and I'd like to have her. The unit I'm renting in Hamilton has a decent garden—with walls around it, so she'll be quite safe. And I promise I'll love her and take great care of her.'

With a slight quaver in her voice, Mrs Firth said, 'Oh, Emma, would you do that? I feel as though I'm abandoning her.'

'Nonsense. Much as we love them, dogs are not as important as daughters.'

'I know, I know, it's just that—oh, don't be kind to me, Emma, or I'll burst into tears! I don't suppose you'd board Lucky too, until this baby is born and Pippa can cope on her own? Of course I'll pay you! My son-in-law wants me to live with them, but he's not very fond of dogs. Once the baby's born I'll find a house of my own close by and send for Lucky—'

'I don't mind looking after Lucky in the least,' Emma said, and took some of the sting from Kane's remark by telling Mrs Firth about it, ending with, 'So perhaps I should set up as the canine equivalent of a nanny!'

Laughing a little, the older woman said, 'Any dog would

be very lucky to have you as its nanny. Emma, thank you so much! You've taken a great weight off my mind. I can deal with this situation much more easily now that I'm not fretting about the dogs.'

When she'd hung up Emma observed to the two interested dogs, 'Well, chaps, it looks as though you've got me for longer than you expected!'

The telephone rang again, making her jump. 'Hello,' she said, assuming it to be Mrs Firth with something she'd forgotten to say.

Instead it was Kane. 'It's too wet to ride,' he said after greeting her. 'Are you all right down there?'

'Yes, of course. Why?' Emma steadied her voice, hoping that it sounded cool—as cool as his—and competent.

As though that kiss had never happened.

'Because the stream at the back can flood, and there's a heavy rain warning out.'

'I'll keep an eye on it,' she promised.

'Do that, and if the water starts rising above the silver birches, let me know straight away.'

This man, she reminded herself, is engaged to another woman. That protectiveness is simply a part of his nature—the dominant male always looks after his women.

But she wasn't—never would be—one of his women.

Never.

'Thank you,' she said aloofly.

She and the dogs had fun splashing around in the warm rain. The little creek ran high and discoloured, but only swept halfway up the lawn towards the silver birches.

After she'd dried the dogs down Emma ironed clothes and scrubbed the floors in the kitchen and laundry, keeping very busy, trying to convince herself that the gnawing pain in her heart was a temporary aberration.

Barking alerted her to someone's arrival late in the afternoon. At the sight of the dark green car, shining and sleek in the driving rain, Emma's spine stiffened.

She greeted Kane with composure, but he demanded, 'What's the matter?'

'Nothing,' she said, resenting his ability to read her so easily.

'That answer,' he said calmly, 'is a dead giveaway.'

Unable to trust her voice, she shrugged. How dared he look at her like that, amber eyes gleaming, when he belonged to another woman?

The burst of rage this thought inspired gave Emma the impetus to say in a honeyed, reckless voice, 'Have you just come back from Australia?'

His head jerked upwards. A muscle flicked along the lean jawline. Very quietly he said, 'Who told you?'

CHAPTER SEVEN

WHEN Emma didn't answer, Kane said, 'Annabelle.'

'Nobody told me,' Emma returned, each word like a stone in her heart. 'I haven't spoken to anyone at the homestead.'

His tough features were clamped into an expression of unconscious arrogance that fired Emma's resistance. Clamping her mouth steady, she met his glittering gaze with unfaltering pride.

A taut, intimidating silence hummed between them.

Finally he said bleakly, 'I went to Australia to tell the woman I was engaged to that I wanted to break the engagement.'

Hope, intense, liberating, flooded through Emma, shocking her with its power, and beneath it burned a fierce anticipation. She couldn't find words, and Kane went on in a dispassionate voice, 'You must know that I want you.'

Emma's eyes widened. She had to stop this because if he kept talking her life would never be the same again. But no words could force their way past the blockage in her throat.

Still in that forbidding, impersonal tone, he went on, 'I tried to discount the first physical attraction because it means little. Over the years I've wanted other women.'

Emma's hand clenched and she made a small, harsh sound.

A hooded, dangerous look darkened his eyes. 'Just as you've wanted other men. Unfortunately I couldn't dismiss it so easily. I wouldn't let you contact the man whose sheep were killed in case he was rude to you. I made up excuses to see you all the time. I even offered Jennifer's horse to you to ride.'

Emma's mouth opened in a noiseless oh.

'Yes,' he said with open contempt. 'I told myself that it was just a fever in the blood, and eventually it would die. But I thought of you constantly, in spite of the fact that you're so young. And it was very obvious that you didn't damned well notice!'

'I knew you were interested,' she said cynically, 'but, as you said, that doesn't mean anything.'

He looked at her hungrily, the fire in his eyes cold no longer. 'You didn't show any sign of it.'

She should tell him about Diane—right now.

If she did, he'd turn away and leave her and she'd never see him again. Conscience fought a brief, vicious battle with cowardice.

And, although she despised herself, cowardice won. She said huskily, 'It wasn't long before I was daydreaming.'

'How long?'

'A couple of days,' she admitted, terrified, because she'd passed the point of no return. Whatever happened now she was committed to it. By keeping quiet about her part in Diane's past she was burning her bridges. And, oh, she thought on an indrawn breath, they made a lovely fire, those bridges, burning away her past, flaming across her future—or that small part of it she might share with Kane.

He smiled dangerously. 'Good.'

'But you showed no signs—you'd be nice, and then suddenly you'd go all distant. I knew you were engaged or virtually so, of course.'

He frowned. 'Just to set the record straight, there's been no official engagement. But morally—yes. At first I rationalised that this acute and highly inconvenient attraction was purely physical. But that didn't work. I couldn't see enough of you. I'm not normally jealous, but I found myself jealous of Rory, which is why I was so bad-tempered when I told you about the sheep. You were laughing with him, and you'd never laughed like that with me.'

'Because it meant too much,' she said quickly.

His eyes kindled, but he didn't move. 'Yes. But Rory wasn't the only one. I was jealous of the friends who took you for a picnic, even jealous of those bloody dogs because you stroked them and they had the right to be close to you.'

Emma said swiftly, bluntly, 'And I told myself that you were engaged, and you showed no signs of being interested.' Her mouth twisted. 'I tried to convince myself that I wasn't jealous of Annabelle—that I couldn't be jealous of a schoolgirl with a crush! But when she took your arm and leaned against you I could have pushed her away and told her to leave you alone.'

'Yes,' Kane said, showing his teeth in a smile without humour. 'And then I saw you sitting under the elm tree in the sun, with your face lifted and your mouth curved in a little, lazy smile, and I knew it had gone too far for my rationalising. At that moment I didn't care about Jennifer—I didn't care about anything at all but you. So I went to tell her it was over.'

'I'm sorry. It must have hurt you both.'

'It wasn't easy,' he said with gritty endurance. 'Neither was telling my mother.' Meeting Emma's swift glance, he added curtly, 'Jennifer is the daughter of an old friend of hers.'

'No wonder your mother doesn't like me.' Yet in a way it was a relief. Mrs Talbot hadn't made the connection between her stepdaughter and Emma—she'd simply been worried because she saw that Kane was attracted to a woman she probably considered an interloper.

And, in spite of her sympathy for both Jennifer and Mrs Talbot, Emma couldn't prevent a small flicker of forbidden pleasure at the thought of affecting Kane like that. Evenly, keeping her expression under rigid control, she said, 'So where do we go from here?'

'Wherever you want to. But you should know that I'm

not a patient man—not where you are concerned.' He spoke without emphasis, and his eyes were cool and dispassionate, but Emma didn't make the mistake of thinking that he wasn't feeling anything.

She bit her lip. He was offering her an affair. And, oh, she wanted one; at the thought of making love to Kane her bones suffered meltdown.

Some cowardly part of her wanted him to sweep her off her feet with passion so that she didn't have to think of the consequences. She almost winced when she glanced up to meet the collected, inexorable detachment in the splintering amber eyes, in the harsh contours of his face, in the straight line of his mouth.

No, he wasn't going to help her. This was something she had to do on her own.

At least she could have this, she thought as excitement exploded through her. He'd said nothing about love, nothing about marriage—just as well, because they weren't likely to happen. But she could find out what it was like to lie in his arms. Even though they could have no future, she could discover the dark glamour of passion with him.

She was never conscious of making the decision. 'I want you,' she said, and heard the words echo through her soul.

He reached her in one stride. 'It's all right,' he said, his voice low and shaken. He picked up her tense hands and held them to his mouth, the cold aggression in his eyes replaced by warmth, by something that might even have been tenderness if he'd loved her.

'It's all right,' he repeated when she shivered mindlessly at the touch of his lips on her palms. 'I keep forgetting how young you are. We'll just take things as they go. I don't want to put any pressure on you.'

But he had; his raw confession of need had set her alight. She said, 'I'm *not* young—I'm twenty-three.'

'And I'm thirty-four.' He dropped her hands and walked

across to the window, not even noticing when Lucky scrambled up out of his way.

The dog was prepared to give the head male his due meed of deference, Emma thought with a ray of sardonic humour.

She stood on the edge of a precipice; one half of her, the earthy, passionate part she'd never known existed, beckoned her into the unknown, urged her to explore the realms of passion and heated, rapturous hunger. The other half, the sensible, practical half that had kept her heart-whole and virginal until then, stressed caution, restraint, an interval to regain her breath, and strove to erect prudent barriers between her and the risky, secret world of the senses.

Kane said quietly, 'It's a big gap in both years and experience. I feel like a satyr plotting the downfall of some innocent nymph.'

'Are you plotting my downfall?'

Emma saw his mouth quirk. 'I suspect that I am.'

It would be enough. It *had* to be enough, because he wasn't talking about love or commitment. And she didn't want him to; if he did, she'd have to tell him about her part in Diane's past.

And then he'd leave her, empty and disconsolate. Better to take what he offered, because that way at least she'd have memories.

She said, 'Nobody who grows up in this world can be totally innocent. And although eleven years is quite a difference, I don't feel much younger than you.'

Something Fran had said flicked up into her brain. There had been a big age gap between his parents. How big? Buried in Kane's unconscious there must be some trace of that small boy who'd seen his parents' marriage torn apart.

He laughed without humour. 'I certainly feel that much older. Emma, shall we be friends?' He smiled, all emotions mastered so that she couldn't see beyond the glittering tawny light in his eyes.

'I'd like that,' she said, adding candidly, 'Although I don't think it will last long.'

'Long enough,' he said with pain in his voice, 'for you to learn that I'm not a man who uses and discards women.'

She felt extremely sorry for the unknown woman who had been engaged to Kane. Had they been sleeping together? Almost certainly. Did she love him? Oh, yes, Emma thought on an indrawn breath. How could she not?

If he did that to her she'd be devastated—as devastated as Diane had been when Emma had made it impossible for her to marry her father. The old guilt weighed heavily on her shoulders.

Before he could say anything more she asked, 'Would you like a cup of coffee?'

'I'll check that creek bank first,' he said, a gleam of amusement illuminating his face.

Emma's heart thudded noisily in her breast. 'I'll come with you.'

'No, you'll get soaked.'

She said very gently, 'Kane, a little water won't hurt me.'

Heavy-lidded eyes blazing, he returned in a voice that lifted each tiny hair on her skin, 'Emma, I'm trying very hard to be strong and noble and resolute.' The mockery was directed at himself, not her. 'If you get wet you'll have to change your clothes, and to be honest, I'm not sure that I'm proof against that temptation.'

Her mouth opened. 'Oh,' she said, unable to look away. Tension sizzled across the room, collected in a ball of visceral fire, danced a passionate flamenco through every cell in her body.

Emma touched her tongue to suddenly dry lips, and her whole being kindled at the leap of primal need in his gaze as he followed the movement. 'All right,' she said weakly, adding, 'But you should know that I don't respond well to orders.'

'One day,' he said, his smile almost feral with anticipation, 'you can show me just how much you enjoy playing in the water.'

And he strode out, taking Lucky with him.

Half-scared, half-elated, Emma made the coffee and set the tray and put out biscuits.

A month ago she'd never have believed that she'd embark on such an ambiguous, rash adventure. High stakes, she thought, trying to dampen down the expectancy that sent every nerve in her body thrumming—she was gambling for high stakes, tossing her safe, pleasant life like a casino chip, gambling on a future that might take her to the stars.

Or send her headlong to hell.

Enjoy it, she thought recklessly. You don't gain anything in this life without risk.

Then Kane came in, smiling, through the door, and she knew that for her there could have been no other decision. Whatever happened, this would be worth it.

They spent the following hour just talking. It was surprisingly easy; he listened to what she had to say, and if he disagreed they discussed it. Emma knew she was intelligent, but many people took one look at her pretty face and decided she was a lightweight. Kane didn't.

They moved from books to music to sport, to the future of the country, the Internet. Emma discovered that although he visited cities, did business in them, socialised and visited theatres and art galleries in them, he left them without a backward glance.

'Me too,' she said lazily. 'I enjoy staying there for a week or so, but the year I spent in Auckland at polytech was enough for me.'

Yet when she left Parahai she'd be going to Hamilton and living in suburbia, away from Taupo with its beloved lake and the mountains.

Time enough to worry about that when it happened.

She'd lit the fire to relieve the gloom, and both dogs were sprawled in front of it, Babe punctuating their conversation with soft little snores. Outside the wind slashed rain across the windows, but inside all was warm and comfortable.

Except that every time Emma met Kane's eyes an unmeasured tide of exhilaration gathered strength and vigour. He fascinated her. When he put his coffee mug down she thought of the way those lean hands would feel on her skin; she watched the flicker of firelight on the powerfully delineated features, and her gaze lingered on the moulded perfection of his mouth as she remembered how it had crushed hers.

She had been right to wonder about that mouth, she thought, smiling secretly.

He broke the small silence by saying roughly, 'If you're going to look at me like that I'll have to go.'

'Like what?' she murmured, realising too late how provocative and foolish the question was.

'As though you want me to do this,' he said, and got to his feet and came across, tall and dark in the firelit room. He held out his hand and, when she put hers in it, pulled her up and into the cage of his arms.

'I won't sit down with you,' he said, shattering her will with a narrow, compelling gaze, 'because I don't trust myself to get up again. But you've been eating me with your eyes for the last five minutes, and suddenly it's not enough.'

His voice was deep and rich with both irony and passion. He bent and kissed the place where her hair sprang back from her temples, then with a raw sound in his throat found her mouth with his.

Their first kiss had lit the tinder of attraction; this one exploded through her like a thunderbolt, and the only way she could gratify the incandescent passion Kane created with his kiss was to yield to it.

And yield she did, abandoning mind and reason to the primeval magic of his mouth.

Even when he lifted his head and said thickly, 'No, this isn't what I intended,' she clung to him, her strong hands entwined in the cotton material of his shirt, pulling herself into the hard, dangerous excitement of his body.

'Emma,' he said, not pulling away but withdrawing in some subtle, indefinable way so that she felt bereft, cold and lost, 'do you know what you're doing?'

When she didn't move or speak his mouth compressed. 'Don't look at me like that,' he said.

His hands came up to hers, disentangled them, and he turned her around, holding her into the heat of his body with an arm beneath her breasts. His chest was a wall behind her, and his scent, indefinable but the essence of Kane, floated around her—marking her, she thought with a leap of the heart.

Such a chaste embrace wasn't what she wanted, and yet as the rage of hunger ebbed she found she liked it, feeling cherished, almost protected.

'All right?' he asked, after long moments broken only by the soft crackle of the fire.

His voice echoed through her. Shivering, she said, 'Yes.'

He let her go and she walked away and across to the window. The rain had stopped and already the dark pall of clouds was being blown away by a brisk wind from the west—a wind that polished the sky and would leave it crisply blue and clear. Emma clenched a hand on the windowsill, gritting her teeth against the tremors that racked
her.

Kane said, 'I'll go now.'

Without turning her head, she nodded.

'Emma.' When she didn't respond his voice gentled. 'Emma, don't worry.'

'Why should I worry?' she asked, the words wrenched from her. 'I know I'm in good hands.'

'What exactly do you mean by that?'

She knew that she was revealing far more than was safe, yet she couldn't stop herself from saying, 'This isn't new for you. As you said, you've wanted other women, and I suppose you've made love to some of them. I've never felt like this before, and I don't know how to deal with it.'

He asked deeply, 'Haven't you made love?'

She bit her lip. Her virginal state was the result of a decision made years ago, and she was adult enough to realise now that she'd probably only kept her vow because until Kane no man had attracted her enough to persuade her to break it.

'Kisses, a little mild groping,' she said, deliberately crude.

'I see.' His tone revealed nothing, and when she turned his expression was shuttered.

'It happens,' she said, head held high.

He smiled. 'I know. It does make a difference, though.'

'In what way?'

She held her breath as he came towards her and her chin came further up in an unconscious defensive gesture.

He stopped just out of reach and said calmly, 'There's an atavistic pleasure in the thought of initiating a virgin, but the pleasure is tempered by the responsibility. Your decision must have been made after a lot of thought; if we do make love, I don't want you to feel afterwards that you've done it for the wrong reason.'

'Which is?'

His smile was twisted. 'Pressure from me. Emma, I want you very much, but I'm not at the mercy of my hormones. I don't want to tempt you into bed with me against your better judgement, or even use your desire to persuade you. When—if you come to me, it must be without fear or worry or disappointment.'

Looking away, she collected her thoughts before saying in a muted voice, 'I can't pretend not to be uncertain, but—Kane, you must know I want you.'

'It's not enough.'

Colour burned through her skin, then ebbed. Before she could say anything he went on in a voice that was deep and confident, 'Let's just get to know each other. We have plenty of time, Emma.'

'We have less than a fortnight,' she said, the words torn from her. 'Then I go to Hamilton.'

He frowned. 'I thought you lived in Taupo.'

When she explained he said, 'Good. It's that much closer,' took a step towards her and held out his hand.

Emma hesitated, then put hers in it, shivering inwardly as his lean fingers closed over hers. Against the dark competence of his, hers looked small and weak, pale and feminine.

'It's only a couple of hours away by plane,' he said, and lifted her wrist to his mouth, turning it so that the blue veins were exposed to the warm seeking of his lips. 'Relax, Emma. More things are lost by rushing than by patience.'

Which was all very fine, Emma thought a few hours later as she pulled the curtains across to hide the darkness outside, but she didn't feel patient at all. That curious splitting of herself had intensified—while the sober, cautious, virginal half of her agreed with Kane, the other part, the Emma she didn't yet know, wanted to plunge headlong into the fire and burn in ecstasy. Even though she knew that she'd have to pay for her recklessness and for the unwitting pain she'd caused Jennifer.

But he was right.

And her blood flowed swiftly, turbulently through her at the prospect of the days ahead.

Spring, she decided a week later, was her favourite season. Dreamily she hugged herself as she gazed at the row of magnolias marching down the hillside opposite, their canopies a magnificent tapestry of cream and pink, each heavily petalled flower cupping a potent measure of perfume in its heart.

The perfect setting for an idyll.

For the past week she'd spent at least part of each day with Kane, learning the lights and shadows of his personality. He liked oysters and fiery Thai food, she'd discovered, and reading murder mysteries, which he treated like crossword puzzles, as well as an enormous number of nonfiction books. He'd begun to ride before he could walk. At school he'd fenced—even though he was the wrong build—and played rugby and squash. When he left school he'd stopped the fencing, but she thought it was probably that which had given him his smooth, lithe grace.

He admired the first Duke of Wellington—as a soldier, not as a politician—and Florence Nightingale and John Donne, the clergyman poet.

He was kind. Emma had been with him when he stopped the car to talk to Davy, who was riding his bike down the road. She'd seen the boy's eyes light up, and his open adoration of the man.

And Davy wasn't the only one. People respected Kane because he was the alpha male, the dominant one, his personality a forceful combination of magnetism and intelligence and a strength buttressed by determination and mellowed by compassion.

Which made it all the more dazzling that he seemed as fascinated by her as she was by him. Although he rarely touched her, and never made his feelings obvious, she basked in the full weight of his attention, as penetrating as a searchlight.

Each morning they'd ridden over the station. He was showing her his heritage, and slowly she'd begun to appreciate his love for this piece of land and what it represented to him.

Once he'd taken her to a lonely white beach, and they'd walked along the hard-packed sand while a vigorous westerly wind buffeted them both, and waves, stained with sand and seaweed, crashed in a thunderous roar, tossing white veils of spume high into the air.

Exhilarated, over-stimulated, Emma had run along the packed white sand, revelling as the wind ripped her hair into shreds, driven slightly crazy by the wild pulse of life throbbing through her.

Kane had laughed, and she'd laughed too, and he'd said in a voice that matched the sea's untamed energy, 'You certainly don't look like Snow White now. You look half-wild, a sea-witch delighting in her power.'

The hot, sexual promise in both voice and eyes flamed through her with the impact of a vow spoken at midnight, of a warning written in tears.

Dizzily she asked, 'What power?'

'The power to enchant,' he said, and took her hand and held it in his big, warm one until they got back to the car. 'To fascinate, to cast spells...'

They ate a picnic lunch in the lee of a thick patch of bush, where the tiny wine-dark flowers of native trees perfumed the air with honey and musk. Although Emma would never remember what they ate she knew she'd never forget the way the sun lingered on Kane's strong features, and the burnished gold of his eyes as they talked. After they'd finished the coffee he stretched out.

'Are you tired?' she asked, stopping a yawn herself.

'I was up last night with a sick cow,' he said, lashes drooping peacefully over his eyes.

She said, 'You'd be more comfortable if you used my lap as a pillow.'

'Innocent Emma,' he said, the gravelly note in his voice sending little rivulets of fire through her.

Again his hand sought hers, and she didn't move for the hour that he slept, instinctively aware as she watched him that this was somehow more precious than anything else that had happened. Joy, so intense that it balanced on the brink of pain, pierced her.

Like a dark shadow, Diane hovered on the edge of her consciousness, as did the knowledge that this was an interlude—sooner or later she'd have to tell Kane about her part in his half-sister's life, and things would never be the same again—but she refused to concede any ground to fear.

She'd made the decision and she was mature enough to deal with the consequences of her actions.

Several times during that week they'd gone out to dinner, but not in Parahai, although the village had good restaurants.

He had no privacy, she'd thought when they went out the first time to a small town some thirty miles up the coast. When you were the most important person in the district everyone was interested in what you were doing.

That night, as they'd eaten fish freshly caught an hour earlier, she'd wondered aloud why a world-class chef was living in a tiny seaside village.

'Because it's the most beautiful place he's ever seen,' Kane said, his voice amused, almost indulgent. 'He came here one day fresh off the plane from Germany and saw a woman and the view, and that was it for him. He's been married for three years and I've never seen a happier man.'

'How romantic,' Emma said breathlessly, because Kane was watching her and there was nothing amused or indulgent about his eyes. Their controlled fire branded her mouth, the smooth skin of her neck and shoulders, the soft swell of her breasts beneath the material of her discreet dress. She felt her breasts grow heavy, the nipples tighten, and sensation scorched down a secret pathway from them to the hidden passage of her womanhood.

But neither that night nor any other did he touch her.

During that week Emma lived in a golden haze of enchantment; she saw Annabelle's resentment and felt sorry for her, but her own emotions—and Kane's—took priority. And although she responded to Rory's teasing with smiles and a quick answer, his slightly malicious amusement couldn't touch her.

She did worry about Jennifer, wishing that this tremulous, inchoate joy hadn't been built on another woman's unhappiness. But as the days went on she began to forget the unknown woman, began to forget his sister, began to forget everything but the delight of being with Kane.

And, although she knew she was being foolish, she allowed herself to hope. Perhaps Kane would understand that seven years ago she'd been a distraught girl grappling with the realities of her mother's death and the painful knowledge that her father intended to replace his wife with a woman he'd been having an affair with for years. Perhaps Diane was living happily now with someone else.

And—the cruellest, sweetest hope of all—perhaps there was a future for Kane and her.

The only flaw in this time of discovery was his mother. Mrs Talbot was never anything less than polite—she made Emma welcome, she smiled at her and talked to her—but the superlative manners hid a wary reserve.

It hurt that Kane's mother didn't like her.

Especially as she could see how close mother and son were. She wondered whether Mrs Talbot would have disliked any woman who held Kane's interest, but dismissed the thought almost before it had been born, because the older woman had liked Jennifer.

It was a measure of Emma's bemused happiness that it no longer worried her that Mrs Talbot might have made the connection between her stepdaughter and the woman for whom her son had broken his engagement.

Some day, Emma decided now, as she turned away from her rapturous scrutiny of the avenue of magnolias, that ravishing symbol of a love that hadn't lasted, she might be able to convince Mrs Talbot that her son's happiness was safe with her.

Because, although neither she nor Kane ever alluded to her departure, she knew that going back to Hamilton wouldn't signal the end of their relationship.

From the corner of her eye she caught a movement beneath the magnolias. Excitement curled lazily in the pit of her stomach. Yes, there was Kane's car. Singing, she danced her way through the house, stopping to talk to the dogs.

'We're going out to an auction this morning,' she said,

stroking Babe's head, 'and we'll be home about two. I'll play with you both then and take you out for a w-a-l-k. You, my boy—' as she fondled an importunate Lucky's ears '—are getting fat, so we'll do an extra mile or so with you after we've brought Babe home.'

Bending, she ran her hand along his back. He was certainly packing on weight, and although she'd cut back his meals as yet he hadn't lost any of that extra cushion over his ribs.

'And after we've done that, you'll be good and tired when Kane and I go out. We'll be having dinner at his place, so we won't be late. Be good now.'

She'd been a little uneasy, a little self-conscious about the prospect of eating dinner at Glenalbyn, but it was a delicious meal, and a pleasant enough evening in spite of Annabelle's angry face and curt manners.

Halfway through dinner Mrs Talbot asked, 'How is Mrs Firth getting on in Vancouver?'

'I think she likes it.'

Kane's mother finished eating a spear of asparagus. 'Her daughter is there, isn't she?'

'Yes. Pippa's husband is a Canadian.'

'I heard that she wasn't well?'

Emma nodded.

'And also,' Mrs Talbot pursued, 'that Mrs Firth has decided to sell up and stay there.'

'Ah, that explains the land agent's car in there this afternoon,' Rory said negligently.

In the country nobody missed anything! It was the reverse of the help so freely offered when things went wrong. Well, everyone would know soon enough, so Emma said, 'Yes. She came to look at the place.'

Leaning forward, Annabelle asked, 'So that means you'll be going soon?'

'Very soon,' Emma said gently.

Clearly 'very soon' was not soon enough for Annabelle,

but after a swift, sideways glance at Kane, whose expression hadn't changed throughout this polite interrogation, the younger woman went back to pushing her spears of asparagus around her plate.

To Emma's relief, Mrs Talbot introduced another topic of conversation.

After dinner Kane wanted to watch a documentary he'd videoed about world trade patterns. It was, Emma realised exultantly, a tiny step forward in their relationship. He was not treating her as a guest; she was part of the family. That sweet, painful hope stirred, and with it the ever-present fear, because sooner or later she'd have to tell Kane about Diane.

'Oh, boring stuff,' Rory said. 'I'm going to bed, if you don't mind.'

Although Kane lifted his brows, he said mildly enough, 'Goodnight.'

But Annabelle decided to watch it with them. Halfway through it Emma woke to Kane's amused voice.

'As Rory said, dull stuff,' he commented. 'Come on, Sleeping Beauty, I'll take you home.'

'Wrong fairy tale,' she said, embarrassed and pink as she stifled a yawn.

Curled up on the big sofa, Annabelle watched her with malicious eyes and said, 'Perhaps it should be the little goose girl.'

Emma gave her a vague smile, but Kane ignored her totally, and Annabelle's face stiffened. Poor kid, Emma thought, allowing him to pull her to her feet.

On the way home, he said, 'You're very quiet. Not letting Annabelle's crack get to you, I hope?'

'No. I feel sorry for her. I had a violent crush on a locum at the vet clinic when I was sixteen, and suffered the tortures of the damned when I found out...' Her voice trailed away. She'd been going to say 'when I found out he was married', but it seemed too presumptuous, so she finished, 'That he wasn't in the least interested in me. Actually, I was thinking that in five days' time I'll be in Hamilton.'

Quietly, his voice even and unruffled, he said, 'Give me your address and telephone number when we get home. And Hamilton's not that far away, Emma.'

'You're used to flying around the world on business trips! To me it seems a long, long way.'

She wanted the reassurance of his touch, while knowing that he wouldn't give it. She was wrong. His hand dropped over hers and held them tightly for a moment before moving back up to the steering wheel.

'Miss me just as much as I'll miss you,' he said, 'but don't worry. We'll be seeing a lot of each other.'

And that was all she needed. Bright with faith, with trust and the prospect of joy, the future beckoned her on, so much so that for a moment she didn't realise what Kane was saying.

'...I'm interested in buying her house,' he finished.

'Mrs Firth's?'

'Yes.' He sounded amused, as though he knew exactly what effect his implied promise had had on her.

Emma waited, but he didn't say why. She murmured, 'I'll tell her that.'

'How will you organise the dogs?'

'I'll take them with me. Babe will stay permanently; she's too old to emigrate—she'd pine away in quarantine. And I have to find out the Canadian regulations for Lucky.' She'd meant to do it that week, but there had been no hurry, and her mind had been full of other things.

She'd never been one to procrastinate, so it just went to show how Kane had scrambled her brain. I'll do it tomorrow, she vowed.

When the car stopped at the gate Kane said, 'You should keep Lucky too. He's bonded so well with you he might find it difficult to attach himself to Mrs Firth again.'

Emma, who'd been worrying about this, said, 'I'd like to have him, but we'll face that when we have to.' She began to open the door.

'I'll do the gate,' he said. 'Those shoes were not made for walking on gravel.'

An absurd little glow of pleasure suffused her. Although she'd worn an extravagantly expensive pair of shoes because they showed off her slim ankles and narrow feet, she hadn't really expected him to notice.

He drove up to the house and turned the engine off, saying into the silence, 'Five days seems far too short.'

Before she could answer he leaned over and kissed her, taking her surprised mouth with a controlled ferocity that called forth a matching need from her. Ignoring the discomfort of the steering wheel, she strained close to him and gloried in the pressure of his mouth on hers, the wild masculine taste and the accelerating thunder of his heartbeat against her palms.

Eventually he lifted his head and kissed her eyes closed, and then the edge of her temple where her hair sprang back from her forehead, and the curl that encircled her ear, and finally the tender hollow just below her ear.

Emma had heard of erogenous zones. She even knew that there was one just there. What she hadn't read was that when one man's lips lingered there, when he touched that sensitive spot with the tip of his tongue, everything inside her would reach flashpoint and she'd ignite like kindling, burnt by a divine fire.

'I'd better get you inside,' he said unsteadily, his voice reverberating through her head and her heart.

CHAPTER EIGHT

IT WAS raining again, soft rain this time, and warm, but Kane sheltered Emma with his arm when they ran to the back door, and in the gentle discretion of the darkness he turned her and kissed her again, and she thought frantically, I can't bear this, I can't *bear* it…

Until he lifted his head and said, 'Not a good idea,' with a note that came close to anger threading the words.

He stepped back so he wasn't touching her as she tried to unlock the door, but he sensed her startled stillness. 'What is it?'

'It's unlocked,' she muttered. 'Not open—just unlocked. And I distinctly remember locking it before I came away.'

'Wait!'

But she'd already pushed it open and been greeted by a cheerful Lucky. Kane pushed past and made sure he was ahead of her when they went inside.

So he saw it first. On the floor behind the sofa, as though it had been slung over the back and fallen. Nothing much—a jacket of supple, expensive suede, black and sleek.

'Is that yours?' Kane asked in a low monotone, checking the room in one swift, lancing scrutiny. 'Or the land agent's?'

Her gaze fixed to the jacket, Emma recalled the land agent. In her mid-fifties, she'd worn an elegant dark green suit. 'No,' she whispered.

'I'll go through the house, but I doubt if anyone's here.'

No one was. Back in the sitting room, Kane went down on one knee and examined the garment, lean fingers carefully going through the empty pockets. 'Who else has a key to this place?' he demanded, getting to his feet after the fruitless search. 'Apart from Fran?'

'Mrs Firth's solicitor, but that doesn't look like anything to do with a solicitor.' The butterflies in Emma's stomach threatened to transmute into something much nastier.

'The land agent?'

'Not yet.'

He walked back to the door, his frown deepening as he examined the lock. 'A hardware shop special,' he said disgustedly. 'Any high school kid could get keys to open this. Get some clothes and a toothbrush—you're coming home with me.'

Although Emma wanted nothing more than to leave the house and go with him, she shook her head. 'I can't,' she said. 'What if whoever owns this comes back and trashes the house? I couldn't let that happen to Mrs Firth.'

'And what if he comes back while you're here?' he enquired grimly.

The thought of Mrs Firth—already worried sick about her daughter and unborn grandchild—hearing that her house had been wrecked made Emma stubborn. 'I can't go,' she said. 'Tomorrow I'll get someone to come out and change all the locks—'

'And if he comes back tonight?' Kane asked relentlessly.

Although Emma had to steady her voice and stiffen her backbone, she said evenly, 'The dogs will let me know if anyone's around. I wonder if they already have... But it probably wasn't anything.'

'What the hell are you talking about?'

'The dogs barked.' Colour tinged her pale skin. 'The evening after you kissed me the first time—I was sitting in front of the fire and they pricked up their ears and looked at the window, then when I went into the kitchen to make myself some chocolate they barked and ran towards the back door. I was a bit scared because the security light came on, but no one was there.'

'Did you go out?' His words split the silence with the sharp impact of gunfire.

'No. I called out and switched the lights on inside.'

His brows drew together. 'Had you been sitting in the dark?'

She nodded. 'I was thinking,' she offered lamely.

Kane gave her a hard look, a look she met with lifted chin. 'You and me both,' he said, and added smoothly, 'I could pick you up and carry you out of here.'

Emma was horrified at the swift kick of desire the cool statement summoned. Her breath came unevenly as heat licked across her nerves and up through her skin. Nevertheless she said, 'Brute force no longer works in this world, Kane.'

'It works,' he returned cynically. 'It's just not politically correct. All right, if you won't come with me, I'll stay here.'

'What?'

A cold smile didn't soften the straight line of his mouth. 'You heard. That's your choice. Come home with me or have me stay the night here.'

Biting her lip, Emma stared at his implacable face. Her heart was tumbling in free-fall, stifling any sensible thought before it had a chance to be born.

'There's absolutely no need for you to stay,' she eventually said. 'The dogs—'

'Emma, whoever left that jacket is going to work out where it is and that he could possibly be traced through it.' And forestalling her next remark, he added, 'We have to assume he's got a key.'

She nodded.

Kane went on, 'He's obviously made friends with the dogs—otherwise he wouldn't be confident enough to come inside. Most people treat Rottweilers with great circumspection, so whoever this is knows he's got nothing to fear from Lucky.'

The dog's tail thumped enthusiastically.

'It could be a woman,' Emma said. She looked at Lucky and finished heavily, 'Kane—could it be Davy? He's great friends with the dogs. And Fran has a key. He might think that Lucky is lonely when I'm out and come to see him.'

Kneeling beside the jacket again, Kane turned it slightly so that she could see the label. 'Fran can't afford expensive leather jackets from fashionable shops. And Davy's not a thief.'

'No, of course he's not,' she said hastily. 'I didn't mean that—just that he loves the dogs.'

'Fran keeps a close watch on Davy—I doubt whether he'd be able to go for jaunts at night without her finding out. As for being a woman—this is not a woman's coat. Not unless she's as big as most men in the shoulders.'

He stood up and looked at her with hard, implacable eyes. Emma stared back, her brain refusing to work. Kane wasn't going to go away. She could object all night, but he was going to stay.

'There's a remote chance that it might be Davy,' Kane said, glancing down at the jacket with eyes burnished and opaque as old gold. 'Fran could have been given the jacket for him, and I know he desperately wants a dog. He could have slipped in to play with them while you were away. If it is him, he needs to be taught that it's wrong. Catching him red-handed will do it.'

Unspoken words hovered between them. *And if it isn't Davy, I'll deal with whoever it is.*

Emma sought comfort from Lucky, her fingers absently fondling his ears. No sane intruder would return. He'd have to batter his way in, so Kane would be quite safe. A spark of excitement sizzled along her nerve pathways because Kane was going to sleep in the next room to hers.

'If you really feel it's necessary,' she said reluctantly.

'I'll run the car inside,' he said, accepting her surrender with no comment. 'Just as well it's a double garage.'

'Why not leave it out?' she asked. 'It would be a deterrent.'

'I'd rather catch him.' He looked distinctly pleased at the prospect, his dark warrior's face honed with a purely male anticipation of battle.

Emma's breath lodged somewhere in her throat. Torn between Mrs Firth's situation and Kane's safety, she jettisoned the older woman's peace of mind without a qualm. 'I'll go with you to the homestead.'

Satisfaction burned in his eyes like shards of sunlight imprisoned in ice. 'That's the best idea you've had all night. Get some clothes.'

But during this last week she'd come to know him too well. She said slowly, 'You're going to come back here and wait for him.'

He didn't lie. 'Yes.'

As swiftly, with as much determination, she said, 'In that case I'll stay.'

'I'd feel happier if you were at the homestead.'

She was already shaking her head. 'Do you really think I'd just go tamely back there and wait? No.'

'Be sensible—' he began, stopping when she interrupted him with heated, tumbling words.

'Kane, I'm not going. If you strong-arm me up to the homestead I'll tell your mother what's happened here and make her ring the police.'

After a short, tense silence he said, 'All right, you can stay on one condition,' and he smiled humourlessly when she narrowed her eyes. 'If he comes back, you'll keep out of the way.' Before she could answer he went on, 'Promise me that, or I'll take you home and tie you to a bed until I get back. And my mother will do as I say.'

Outraged, she glared at him, but the flat, inflexible voice and the lethal steadiness of his gaze warned her he meant it.

'I'll keep out of the way,' she said stiffly.

'In your bedroom.'

'Yes.' She clipped the word off short.

He gave her a keen look and said softly, 'I'll be very angry if you don't, Emma.'

'I'm not a child,' she flared. 'Don't you treat me like one, or I'll march straight through there and ring the police now and hand the whole business over to them.'

He said patiently, 'If you do that your call will go through to Auckland, and it'll be at least half an hour before anyone comes. And in that time I'll have you at Glenalbyn if I have to shackle you to my side to get you there.'

They measured glances like swords. Emma vibrated with fury and fear—both for him.

He said quietly, 'Emma, I'm trying bloody hard not to give in to that part of me that wants to get you out of here and keep you safe, no matter how I have to do it. If you were hurt I'd never forgive myself.'

His words, said in a low, dangerous voice, shattered the hold anger had on her. She gave a half-sob and cried passionately, 'That's not fair!'

'Fair or not, it's how I feel.'

Uncompromising, determined, one glance revealed that he'd win by force or subterfuge or reasoned logic—whatever it took. She had no chance of breaking his will, so with rigid reluctance she said, 'Very well, then.'

'Right, I'll put the car in the garage. But first we'll switch off the security light from inside.'

He did this, then picked up the electronic gadget that opened the garage door and went out. Back in the sitting room, Emma sank down into a chair, waiting tensely, a protective Lucky in front of her. Babe yawned and made her way across to her basket.

Neither barked, and almost as soon as she'd sat down Emma got up again. From the cupboard in the hall she took linen to make up Mrs Firth's bed.

Because it might not be a good idea to turn the light on in there she did her best by the dim glow from the sitting room, but was only halfway through when Kane appeared in the doorway, silent and big and intimidating.

'What are you doing?' he asked.

Emma's heart jumped. 'What does it look like?' she asked irritably. 'I'm making up a bed for you.'

'Unnecessary,' he said blandly. 'Is there another bed in your room?'

Astounded, she hesitated, then gave a short nod.

'Then I'll sleep there.'

'I don't think—'

'Tough,' he interrupted.

'Has anyone ever told you,' she asked ominously, 'that you're bossy and rude and overbearing?'

There was a moment's silence before he laughed, a low, amused response that set her back on her heels. Tension heightened her responses, sending highly suspect sensations sizzling through each cell.

'Not often,' he said, 'but you can, whenever you like.'

After a fleeting glance at his face, the formidable, hard-hewn features emphasised by the glow of the lights from the sitting room, she regrouped her forces. Like it or not, he was going to spend the night two feet away from her.

'All right,' she said, flattening her voice to pragmatism. 'I'll strip this bed and make up the one in my room.'

While she did this he went around the house, carefully checking each window and door, accompanied by an alert, interested Lucky.

Twenty minutes later she was safely under the duvet, devoutly grateful that Mrs Firth had furnished her guest room with two single beds instead of a double. Sleeping so close to Kane was going to be hell on her yearning heart; if he'd insisted on sleeping in the same bed she wouldn't be able to close an eyelid.

The prospect drove all fear from her. When Kane came in she said, 'It could be Davy, you know. He really does love the dogs—Lucky especially.'

'I know. I'll have to see Fran about getting him a dog.'

'She says the upkeep is too much.'

'I can help there,' he said absently. 'Have you got a spare toothbrush?'

Emma went to sit up, then slid back, hauling the sheets above her shoulders. Although she'd opted for her most concealing nightgown, a granny one with long sleeves and a lace yoke fastened up to the hollow in her throat with tiny pearl buttons, she thought it better to stay where she was.

She said, 'Mrs Firth has a supply. I left one out on the vanity in the bathroom.'

'Thank you.' He picked up a towel and facecloth and left the room.

Turning on her side, away from the other bed, Emma closed her eyes with determination.

She heard him come in, heard the rustle as the bedclothes were pulled back, saw sudden darkness press against her eyelids when he switched off the light. Quietly, he said, 'Goodnight, Emma.'

His total lack of embarrassment filled her with unhappy resentment. If she'd had more experience—if she'd had a lover or two—spending the night in the same room as a man would hold no mystery for her. Kane's coolness revealed his experience. Sleeping with a woman held no novelty for him—although, she thought with a wry smile, sleeping in a different bed probably did!

Lying very still, she breathed with conscious effort, hoping to steady the persistent thudding of her heart. After a while she managed to control it enough to hear his breathing—regular, slow, just as though nothing disturbed him.

And why should it? she thought forlornly.

'If the dogs bark,' he said, his voice level in the still, cool air, 'I want you to call out to them to be quiet. Then stay put.'

'All right.'

Eventually she drifted off into sleep.

She woke to a suffocating pressure across her mouth and

Kane's voice, pitched so low that it reached no further than her ears. 'Quiet!'

Immediately she stopped struggling and lay quiescent, ears straining to hear what he was saying. The hard pressure on her face eased, lifted.

'Someone's just come in the back door,' Kane breathed.

Fear knotted her stomach. She sat up and strained her ears. A slight scrabbling indicated that one of the dogs—Lucky, probably—was moving about, but apart from that there was no sound except the renewed thunder of her heartbeats.

Noiselessly Kane slid through the door of the bedroom. For a man so big, he moved, she thought with a sharp, terrified pang, like a ghost in the night. Frozen, she sat with every nerve and sinew stretched unbearably, wishing she'd rung the police.

And then the dogs began to bark wildly, not quite hiding the sounds of a scuffle.

Emma shot out of bed and ran down the passage, stopping suddenly as she heard a voice croaking, 'All right—get off, get off!'

It wasn't Kane. Relief temporarily paralysed her, until she heard Kane's deep voice call, 'Emma!'

'I'm here,' she said, switching the light on in the sitting room to reveal Kane kneeling beside the sprawled body of a man on the floor.

'Are you all right?' she demanded, for Kane was breathing heavily and the charcoal hair had been tousled.

'Yes.'

She searched his face for signs of any blows, but he was unmarked, and her gaze switched to the man on the floor, now groaning.

Not Davy, was her first thought.

Rory. Her memory dredged up a fragment of an image—Davy talking in the garden. 'Rory likes Lucky too,' he'd said.

Emma yelled a warning as his cousin suddenly lashed

out at Kane, hand held edge-on in the classical martial arts position. It should have hit Kane across the throat, but he blocked the blow with a swift, blurred movement. Both dogs barked furiously, and Lucky rushed in, teeth bared.

'Stay!' Emma shouted. The dog stopped, but continued to growl, and with an almost casual strength Kane flipped Rory over onto his stomach and held him there with an arm efficiently—and painfully—twisted up his back.

Rory swore, his muffled, grunting words ugly and foreign in the quiet, pretty room.

'That's enough,' Kane said, and when the curses continued put an end to them by increasing the pressure until Rory squealed in pain and the dogs barked again.

'Quiet,' Kane commanded, easing off the pressure. 'What are you doing here?'

His answer was another curse. Kane got to his feet, dragging the younger man with him. Rough handling had untucked Rory's black sweatshirt from his dark jeans and rumpled his carefully styled hair. Flushed, his eyes wild, he stared at Lucky, who was still growling, hackles half-lifted and lips drawn back over exposed teeth.

Emma demanded, 'Did you persuade Davy to steal Fran's key?'

He switched his eyes to her, and looked her over with slow insolence. 'Yes.'

'Why did you want it?'

Rory shrugged, then winced as Kane tightened his grip.

'Answer the question,' Kane said in a silky voice that held a world of menace.

'Make me,' he sneered. 'I wasn't doing anyone any harm.'

Kane said, 'Emma, ring the police, will you? Tell them we've got a burglary and attempted rape.'

Rory's mouth dropped open. 'You can't pin that on me,' he shouted indignantly.

'I don't plan to,' Kane said with cold deliberation. 'The police will do it for me. Why else would you be here?'

After a swift look directed at Emma, Rory returned sullenly, 'I came to get my jacket.'

'And why did you leave your jacket here?'

The indignation returned. 'You bloody came home before I expected you to. You said you were going to watch the video, damn you, so that gave me an hour and a half. But you were back here within half an hour. When I heard you coming I had to run. I left the jacket behind and didn't even have time to lock the back door again.'

'And what,' Kane asked with hard, unsparing authority, 'were you doing in this house?'

'I was going to take the Rottweiler.'

Emma's eyes met Kane's. Lucky, sitting on his haunches and looking from one to the other with ears pricked, got up and came over to sit beside Emma.

'Why?' Kane asked with controlled anger.

'I know a pig hunter who reckons Rotties make the best pig dogs around.' He said it too glibly.

'Pull the other,' Kane advised on an icy note of warning.

Rory opened his mouth, but after a fleeting glance at his tormentor thought better of what he'd been about to say.

Kane said dangerously, 'We can stay here all night if you want to, or I can drive you to the police station. If we do it that way your parents will have to know.'

Rory swallowed and hesitated, then said reluctantly, 'Rottweilers are good fighters.'

Sickened, Emma closed her eyes. She was familiar with the trade in fighting dogs—had even seen a few that had been brutalised, almost killed by it.

'Go on,' Kane ordered implacably.

'So I've been feeding him, gaining his confidence. Then tonight Miss Goody Two Shoes here said she was leaving Parahai soon, and you both decided to watch an hour and a half of television, so I knew that I'd probably never get a better chance.'

Kane said, 'If you've been feeding him, why haven't you taken him before now?'

Rory showed his teeth. 'He might obey you, but he won't damned well obey me. He'll let me pat him if I've got food and haven't got a leash, but even when I hide the thing behind my back or in my pocket he seems to know that I've got one and he won't let me near him.'

Emma said, 'Did you buy one?'

'What, and announce to Parahai that I'm going to steal a dog?' Rory sneered. 'No, I uplifted one of the ones Kane has lying around in his barn.'

Lucky would smell the scent of another dog on the leather. And because he disliked walking on a leash he'd make sure Rory didn't get close enough to put one on him.

'So it had to be tonight,' Kane said without expression.

'Yes. Someone's coming—' He stopped.

'Go on.'

Two short words, but if Kane ever spoke to her in that tone, Emma thought with a shiver, she'd freeze to the marrow of her bones.

It affected Rory too. Paling, he stared at Kane, and swallowed. Huskily, unevenly, he said, 'I've got a place to hide him and someone's coming tomorrow to pick him up and take him to Auckland.'

Kane released him. After a swift glance at the door Rory took one step backwards. Not trying to hide his contempt, Kane ordered, 'Don't try it. I'll hunt you down, and you won't like the consequences. Do you enjoy dog fights?'

'God, no,' Rory said, shuddering. 'But I—' He stopped and licked his lips, looking down at the ground.

No one said anything, and after several moments he went on slowly, 'I owe money—gambling debts—to someone who organises them. He's pushing me. I thought if I gave him a dog—Rottweilers are worth big money. It wouldn't pay all my debts, but it would get me off the hook for a while.'

'Why didn't you go to your father?' Kane asked, stone-faced.

Rory shrugged again. 'You know what he's like,' he said

bitterly. 'Anyway, he's already bailed me out a couple of times.'

Another silence, until Rory said in a conciliating tone, 'Look, we'll do a deal, all right? I didn't come here to hurt Emma—I got the key copied so I could feed the dog and make friends with him.'

Nausea rose again in Emma's throat. She said bitterly, 'So that you could betray him.'

'Oh, for God's sake, you can't betray animals! Dogs like fighting—it's natural for them to do it. And it isn't as though Lucky's yours. Anyway, he's probably going to be put down. Dogs that kill sheep always get caught in the end.'

'Did you leave the door open the night Emma first came to dinner?' Kane asked with cold composure, overriding Emma's furious attempt to answer.

Rory shook his head vigorously. 'No, damn it. I didn't know until then that there was a Rottweiler here. It was only when everyone started to talk about him that I got the idea.'

He sounded sincere, and Emma for one believed him, although it hurt to realise that *she'd* made it possible for the dogs to get out that night.

After a quick glance at Kane's dark face, Rory said eagerly, 'Look, we've got a deal, all right? You can't have me for anything other than breaking and entering, and you know it. I'll leave the dog alone and we'll forget all about it.'

Kane forestalled Emma's angry rejection. 'Give me the key,' he commanded.

Rory fished around in his pocket and drew it out, handing it over to Kane. 'Now can I go?' he asked, with a show of shallow jauntiness that grated on Emma's temper.

Kane said, 'I'll deal with you tomorrow morning.'

'I suppose you'll send me back to Auckland with my tail between my legs,' Rory said with an attempt at bravado.

Kane said quietly, 'I need to think about it. And if you

want anything done about that debt of yours you'd better be there when I get up.'

Rory nodded, his febrile eagerness revealing how cleverly Kane had pushed the right button.

Almost shovelling the younger man ahead of him, Kane went out of the room.

Emma stroked Lucky's black head and ears, anger corroding her self-control so that when Kane came back into the room she demanded vehemently, 'How can you just let him go like that?'

'I don't know yet what I'm going to do,' he said.

She said scornfully, 'I suppose you'll pay his debts and save the family honour this time, and when he gets into trouble like that again—as he will; you *know* he will—he'll go looking for another dog to steal.'

He came across and took her cold hands, holding them against his chest so that the warmth of his body enveloped them. 'He sounds as though he's in real trouble this time, and I think he'll be more valuable to the police as a lead than being sent to prison for breaking and entering.'

'A lead to what?'

'To whoever's organising this dog ring, for a start,' he said. 'He's weak, and it seems he could be a gambling addict, but he's my cousin. He needs counselling, and if he's willing I'll back him.'

'And if he's not?'

The warrior's features set into a bronze mask. 'Then he's on his own,' he said.

Emma managed a wobbly smile. 'You wouldn't just dump him.'

Silently he pulled her into the warm hardness of his body and held her tightly, his arms contracting across her back. 'You're shivering,' he said into her hair. 'Would you like me to make you something to drink?'

Emma shook her head. 'It's just reaction. I heard you fighting with him. And then I was so angry with him I could have killed him.'

He lifted her chin and looked at her, and for the first time she saw the cold fire in his eyes unbanked. 'I'm sorry,' he said, and repeated it after a taut moment in a voice that was deep and raw and unguarded.

And then, at last, he kissed her.

Adrenalin must have been pumping through him too, for that kiss had the stark desperation of a man who had reached the end of his tether. He kissed her without regard for her softness, as though he'd been holding back from this for years and could restrain himself no longer.

Emma gasped, then returned the kiss with the dammed intensity of the past week. She made no protest when he picked her up and carried her into the room they'd shared for the first part of the night; with his mouth still on hers, he stooped and slid her between the sheets.

But when he broke off the kiss and began to get up she said urgently, 'No!' and her hands clenched onto the material of his shirt.

'Emma,' he said, his voice harsh and roughly timbred, 'don't make it difficult.'

'What could be easier?' she murmured, devouring him with a heavy, slumbrous gaze.

He bent his head and kissed her hands, his mouth lingering. 'I don't want you to be sorry in the morning,' he said thickly.

Sorry? How could she be sorry, unless he left her? She said, 'I don't want you to go.'

'You're frightened—'

'Oh, Kane, I'm not scared—or only a little bit.' Through the half-darkness she scanned the arrogant, hard-honed features of the man she loved, and went on with ardent conviction, 'I might be several years younger than you are, but I do know what I'm doing.'

'I hope so,' he said, the same fierce determination that had branded his kisses echoing in his tone.

And he kissed her again.

What followed had nothing of finesse—it was not courtship but mating, a wild, erotic coming together.

Occasionally Emma had wondered what making love would be like. She'd hoped that it would be sweet and gentle, that the man she loved would understand her shyness and woo her with tenderness.

There was little gentleness in Kane's lovemaking, or in her response. Later, when she remembered what she'd done, what she'd said, she'd be appalled by her frankness and her hunger, although some part of her recognised that this was how she would always be with Kane—possessed by an untamed, violent drive towards consummation.

His hands stripped away her clothes, and she urged him from his. For long moments he held her, his arms like iron bands, his mouth locked onto the hollow at the base of her throat.

Emma had read of the way young birds were imprinted by the first moving thing they saw after birth—even if it was a person—so that ever after they saw that person as the source of food and protection.

Now, as she breathed air that was impregnated with Kane's faint masculine essence, as she thrilled to the sleek slide of his skin on hers, the rapid, unsteady beat of his heart against her, she thought that he was imprinting her so that there would never be any other man.

But at last he said roughly, 'Emma. Beautiful, bright, passionate Emma. I wanted to see you like this the first time we met.' The words were tiny explosions across skin sensitised by his mouth.

She shivered. 'I didn't know.'

'I'm surprised. I thought I was blatantly obvious.' He kissed her collarbone, and lifted her so that her head and shoulders fell back and he could easily reach her breasts with his ravenous mouth.

The heat of his lips, the rasp of his beard like raw silk on her skin, set off something like an electric shock. Sensation shuddered through her as he kissed the little round nub at the centre of one breast and then drew it into the warm, dark cavern of his mouth.

An odd, garbled murmur blocked Emma's throat. She croaked his name and her body was doused in fire, pierced by slivers of sensation so close to torment that she writhed against him, seeking something to ease it.

She had never thought making love would be like this—uncontained, a primitive triumph, nothing sane or civilised about it.

Opening her eyes at the bunch and coil of his muscles, she watched his face as he lowered her onto the pillow, and his hand slid from behind her to her hip, and then down to the crisp curls that hid the source of her ardour, the driving hunger that he evoked with his mouth and his smouldering male sensuality.

With eyes better attuned to the dimness she saw tautness sharpen the angular features—the only outward sign of the incredible control he was imposing on himself. A hint of panic clouded her mind.

'It's all right,' he said, his voice washing across her skin so that again she felt the words as she heard them. 'Don't be scared. Let me show you how it can be, Emma...'

He showed her. With her mouth under his, he readied her for that final joining by mimicry, almost banishing the fear that lurked at the back of her mind.

Lost in the starstorm of his expertise and her own response, she went with him wherever he led, awed by the latent strength beneath the hot, smooth skin of the shoulders she clutched, only too aware of how helpless she was against that male power.

Yet, in spite of the dangerous force of his passion, she knew he wouldn't hurt her. Oh, there might be pain in this joining, but he wouldn't brutalise her in the many ways a man can when a woman is at her most physically vulnerable.

Dazed by the demanding insistence of his mouth, she saw his eyes turn to sheer gold—hungry eyes that watched her response with smouldering satisfaction. He kissed her other breast, and suckled with lingering enjoyment, an absorbed pleasure he transmitted to Emma. Swiftly, involuntarily, her body arched into him, seeking a closer, more fundamental nearness.

He made a sound deep in his throat and lifted his head. The cool air puckered her nipple and he kissed it, a set, humourless smile curving his lips.

Then he stunned her by making a belt of kisses across her waist. Enchanted, she sucked in her breath, compressing the muscles, a feverish tension plucking at her heartstrings when he found the neat little dimple below it and explored it with excruciating, slow movements of his tongue.

Excitement rode Emma, excitement mixed with a bashfulness which he must have sensed, for he returned to her breasts, lingering over them until she'd lost all remnants of modesty to a driving urgency that built and built and built into a storm of sensation, sweeping the last vestiges of rational thought before it, dissipating sanity to the winds.

Emma heard her strained voice moan his name and reached for him, pulling him down to her.

'Wait a moment,' he said harshly.

She said, 'What—?' before falling silent as she realised what he was doing. Some of the urgency drained from her, but almost immediately he returned to her, and with slow, drugging expertise began to kiss her again.

Soon, when she was panting with frustration and need, he came over her, blocking out the light, and for a moment she froze in primal fear of the unknown, dimly realising that once this was done there would be no going back—she would be a different person.

And then he pushed home, and although that first measured thrust hurt in a strange way, stretching her until she thought she couldn't contain him any more, the slow, relentless invasion appeased for a second the wildness beating through her.

The seeking, passionate hunger he'd roused ebbed a little, overlaid by the reality of his embrace, the sheer male forcefulness of his entry into her tender body, but she knew that this wasn't all there was, and some part of her rebelled, outraged at Kane's control when she had none.

When he began to pull away Emma muttered, 'No!' and slid her arms across his back, desperately holding him in place.

'Wait,' he said, kissing the top of her ear.

The ache in her body sprang from deep in her bones, so close to a fever that she tried to ease it by arching again, her hips rotating instinctively.

'No,' he said, the word curt with authority.

But Emma had heard the sharp intake of his breath, felt the jagged thunder of his heart, and she rejoiced. Again she twisted beneath him, and this time she pressed her mouth to the swell of the muscle on his shoulder, and bit.

As though it had been a signal, he thrust completely into her, setting up a friction that catapulted her into another world, a world where the only things that mattered were purely physical—the harsh rasp of Kane's breath as he finally surrendered the control she'd shattered, their mingled scent, his slick, heated skin beneath her fingers, the force and power of his possession, the ardent welcome of her own body as she enclosed him.

Unhinged by the sensuous assault, Emma cried out at the mixture of honey-sweet sensation and clamorous compulsion that assailed her. After a few moments she found a rhythm as old as woman, as old as sex, and began to rise with each movement, unfettered desire driving her up to orgasm.

Waves spread through her—breakers, fierce, almost impersonal—tossing her ahead and into an unknown place where there was only Kane, and her response to his primal sexuality, his need to mate and spill his seed.

The last of the waves caught her by surprise, flinging her through force fields of energy, of bliss beyond imagination. Wholly caught up in rapture, she let the waves take her where she wanted to go, and when at last the rapturous delight began to fade into sleepy, sated languor, Kane thrust more heavily and faster, and as she forced her eyelids up she saw him fling his head back, saw the cords on his throat stand out and heard his deep groan of ecstasy.

CHAPTER NINE

LIMP, exhausted, Emma lay on some tropical beach of spent desire as tiredness rolled over her. Kane's weight was as precious as the passion he'd given her, his lax body mirroring her lethargy until he lifted himself on his elbows and turned, taking her with him so that she finished lying half on his chest. Long fingers threaded through her hair, gently pulling her face back so that he could look at her.

'Are you all right?' he asked.

She gave an uncertain smile. 'Yes.'

'You screamed,' he said.

Until that moment she had forgotten the sound torn from her throat as she'd convulsed beneath him. Heat scorched her skin. 'I know. I'm sorry. It didn't hurt—I didn't know I was going to.'

He dropped a hard kiss on her mouth, but when he spoke his voice was sombre. 'I should have stopped, but I couldn't.'

'I'd have killed you if you had,' she said, turning her face against the turbulent thudding of his heart to enjoy the silky friction of his hair on her cheek.

His chest lifted. To her astonishment she heard him laugh. 'You're a constant joy,' he said, and for the first time, she thought deliriously, he was speaking to her as an equal, not as a woman eleven years younger than he was, a woman to be protected and cosseted.

'Because I enjoyed making love with you?'

'Because you look like Snow White and you behave like a modern woman.'

'We've had this conversation before,' she murmured. 'Snow White had guts; she used what assets she had to survive, and she worked hard and got her reward. A very modern woman.'

'Am I your reward?' he asked, the amusement in his voice mixed with a wry note.

She laughed. 'Don't you want to be?'

'What I want,' he said deliberately, 'is probably not something I should be thinking about.'

'Why? Because I'm younger than you are?'

His free hand came up and cupped her breast. Emma looked down, her bones melting at the primitive contrast of dark skin against white, strength against soft, nurturing curves.

Her sated body quickened, and she drew in a sharp breath as she realised that he too was recharged, energy flickering around him like lightning against the hills.

Without a word she touched his chest, running her fingers through the tangled hair, following the classical pattern it made across the breadth of his chest and down his midriff. Remembering the excitement that had surged through her when he'd kissed her there, Emma wriggled down and set her mouth just above the small indentation of his navel. He tasted salty—salt with a musk flavour, she thought.

'No,' he said harshly, and pulled her up to lie on his chest.

'Why?'

His amber eyes glittered. 'If you touch me I'll take you again, and you're not ready for that.'

Relief and a kind of gratitude flooded her. He was right; she could feel a tender ache between her legs, and said wistfully, 'No.'

His arms closed around her. In a voice muffled by her hair he said, 'It doesn't matter.'

'I didn't realise,' she said honestly, 'that it's possible for a woman to climax the first time. You're a brilliant lover.'

'You don't think that it's because you trust me?'

'Of course I trust you,' she said. 'If I didn't trust you I wouldn't have made love.'

His smile sent a tiny shiver the length of her spine. 'Is that why you responded so passionately? Because you trust me?'

Emma looked into eyes that burned with a savage, cold fire, features that were marked with a warrior's brand. So this is what love is about, she thought wonderingly.

And yet—was it love, or was it the afterglow of wonderful sex?

Kissing the side of his mouth, she murmured, 'And because I wanted—want—you.'

It was almost as though he relaxed, as though he'd made some sort of decision. 'Still?' he asked slowly, his eyes focusing to an almost hypnotic intensity.

Emma's skin tightened as a surge of desire heated her flesh. 'Yes,' she said huskily. 'I still want you, damn you. What are we going to do about that?'

'Oh, I think I can deal with it,' he said, lowering his head to coax her mouth open beneath his.

An hour later Emma lay back in her own bed, so close to sleep that she couldn't think straight—her mind kept drifting off into reveries that made her shiver. Kane had made love to her with skill and erotic expertise, he'd brought her to ecstasy several times, yet he hadn't taken her again, or let her touch him. He'd given her paradise—and the memory made her feel degraded.

Why? With gritted teeth she forced the clinging, seductive exhaustion back. If she didn't think this through now she'd wake tomorrow with her memories smeared by an unknown reaction, one she could no longer contact.

He'd been gentle, taking exquisite care not to hurt her, not to offend her; he'd shown her ways of making love that had left her trembling and breathless with excitement and ardour. That fierce intensity of concentration had been exciting in itself; he'd focused completely on her responses, on her needs.

And that, she realised now, with her mind unhazed by passion, was her problem: hidden behind his dazzling, skilful lovemaking had been an odd detachment. Oh, he'd wanted her, but he'd managed to master his desire so there was nothing of the forceful, unmanageable urgency of that first wild mating.

She couldn't feel used, she thought, frowning into the night, because that was untrue. And yet...

He'd shown her the gates of paradise and he'd left her there, still supplicant outside, still longing for something she would probably never have.

Kane's love.

But you don't even know that you love him, she told herself caustically. You're probably suffering from post-coital blues, crying for a moon that doesn't exist...

She'd have liked them to share a bed, even though he'd take up most of the space, but he'd made it obvious he intended to sleep on his own. Listening to the regular rise and fall of his breath, Emma thought that he might have lost his head during that first impassioned lovemaking, but he'd regained it very quickly. The separate beds were an indication of how he saw them—two essentially separate lives.

Emma had never felt so alone in all her life.

In the end, after a long, bleak time spent wooing it, sleep swallowed her up.

She woke late, unsurprised to see that Kane had gone; his bedclothes had been pulled down to the bottom of the bed and the sun had risen far enough to glow through the curtains, which meant it was after eight o'clock.

Life had to go on. She might want to stay in bed, greedily recalling the previous night, but the dogs, she thought grimly as she got up, would be starving. So she hurried into the warm comfort of her dressing gown before leaving the bedroom without a further glance at the bed where Kane had spent the night.

The house was empty except for two lazy dogs. Anchored to the kitchen bench by a pepperpot was a note.

'Had to go home,' it read. 'I'll be back at ten o'clock. I've fed the dogs and given them a run.'

He'd written it with the ballpoint pen Mrs Firth kept by the telephone to take messages with, but the smooth flow of ink couldn't soften the forceful writing.

No salutation, no farewell—not even a signature. The unease that had gripped Emma the night before crystallised into panic. What had happened? She'd heard of men for whom the hunt was the attraction; after sex they lost interest. But it was impossible to believe that Kane was like that.

There were men—psychologically disturbed—whose great interest lay in initiating virgins. Not Kane, she thought, her hands gripping the edge of the bench. No, not Kane!

Perhaps he thought that she didn't understand the rules, the conventions that governed affairs. Did he fear that she might expect him to marry her?

Her mouth pulled into a bitter smile. She'd need to be stupid to fall into that trap. He'd never said anything about love, after all.

What had happened? She sat down at the small breakfast table and tried to remember exactly what she'd said just before he'd retreated.

She'd told him that she trusted him, and that he was a brilliant lover. Had she seemed too gauche for a man as experienced and sophisticated as Kane Talbot?

A kind of humiliation made her cringe. Lucky whined and thrust his head under her hand, and as she stroked him and told him what a good dog he was she remembered that Rory—nice, amiable, snobbish Rory, with his expensive little sports car and top label clothes, and his family business to walk into—had planned to sell Lucky to people who'd force him to fight against other dogs, a practice that would brutalise and eventually kill him, all for their own sick pleasure.

And for money, she thought grimly. Let's not forget the money!

'Oh, Lucky,' she said, trying to hold the tears back.

He whined, and licked her wrist, and a soft scritch-scritch of claws preceded Babe, drawn by the age-old bond between humans and the first animals ever domesticated.

A good cry was supposed to help you feel better. It didn't do anything for Emma beyond making her eyes red and giving her the beginnings of a headache. Eventually she stopped and got up. She had work to do, and she'd have to be back at the house by midday because that was when Mrs Firth was going to ring and tell her exactly what she'd planned.

As though in answer to her thought, the telephone shrilled an imperative summons.

Not Mrs Firth, which meant it would only be one person. Sure enough, Kane asked curtly, 'Can you come up immediately?'

'Yes, of course,' she said numbly, adding, 'In about half an hour.'

'I'll see you then.'

He'd sounded brusque and angry, so no doubt he wanted to talk to her about Rory.

It took her twenty minutes to shower and do all the other necessary things, to dress in jeans and a shirt and a fine woollen jersey in a clear, clean pink that gave a little colour to her pale skin.

Carefully she brushed her hair, pulling it back from her face in an attempt to make herself look older. It failed—she didn't have the chiselled features that could cope with such severity. Anyway, her hair wouldn't *be* severe; tiny curls escaped and fringed her face, reducing her once more to mere prettiness.

'Damn,' she said fretfully, and outlined her tender mouth in lipgloss.

Last night...

'No!' she said, so angrily that both dogs sat up and stared at her.

With a hollow emptiness beneath her breastbone, she put them in the car and drove up to the homestead.

Her hands were trembling. She parked the car and switched off the engine, wound down the windows so that the dogs were able to breathe, then locked it and put the keys in her bag. Stray, terrified thoughts jostled in her brain.

What is the matter with you? she demanded, furious with herself for such a reaction. Did every woman feel so—so *bereft* the first time they made love? She was overreacting and she could just stop it. Right now.

Shoulders stiff, spine straight, she walked over the gravel forecourt and knocked at the main door of the homestead.

The housekeeper opened it. 'Hello,' she said cheerfully. 'Isn't it a glorious day? Come on in—they're all in the morning room.'

And they all were—Kane standing in the window, tall and dark with the sunlight striking flames from his hair, the hard face set in lines of cold control; Mrs Talbot getting to her feet, her lovely face at once alarmed and complacent; and another woman.

Emma could see the resemblance between the newcomer and Kane. That hint of familiarity when she'd met Kane had been based on hair the same colour, so dark it could be called black until the sun summoned its latent fire, and features that were softened and feminised in his half-sister.

'Hello, Emma,' Diane Heathcote said. 'I've often wondered how you grew up. I'm surprised at how little you've changed.'

It took only one glance to reveal that Mrs Talbot had arranged this, or at the very least had known of her step-daughter's imminent arrival. Which meant, of course, that she also knew what had happened seven years ago.

Emma braced herself. She could deal with that later. She said steadily, 'Hello, Diane.'

'Your father's dead, isn't he?' Diane asked.

'Yes.'

Diane briefly closed her dark eyes.

Ignoring the silent man in the window, Emma dragged in a deep breath. 'I know it's far too late, but I'd like to apologise for the way I behaved then.'

'You're right, you conniving little bitch,' Diane said with silky violence, 'it is far too late. How many other women did you run off before he died?'

'That's enough,' Kane said harshly.

Emma felt sick; she'd expected Diane's resentment, but it hadn't occurred to her that Diane might still feel something for her lost lover. 'Nobody else,' she told the older woman, adding with enormous reluctance, because she knew how much it was going to hurt, 'He only loved you.'

'I know he loved me, but he wouldn't marry me. He promised—do you know how long I waited? Three years! He couldn't leave your mother, and I understood that, so I waited and tried to be satisfied with the crumbs of his life, but when she died and *you* made it impossible for us—it was all for nothing...'

Emma was aware of Mrs Talbot's appalled face, of Kane's predatory stillness. They hadn't known that Diane had been her father's lover before her mother had died. Struggling for composure, she said, 'I know I did my best to get rid of you, but has it never occurred to you that sleeping with my father when my mother was dying was not the way to endear yourself to me?'

Diane's head jerked upright. Patches of colour staining her cheeks, she retorted harshly, 'She didn't know!'

'She knew,' Emma said, her voice sombre. Forcing the words past a dry, tight throat, she finished, 'I hated you with good reason, I thought, but I shouldn't have lied and cheated. I'm sorry for the pain I caused both you and my father.'

'What use is that to me? He's dead, and if it hadn't been for you I'd have married him, been with him for whatever time he had left! You robbed me, stole that time from me.

I'll never forgive you, and I don't suppose he ever did, either.'

'Diane, that will do,' Kane said, his voice so bleak and controlled that each word was like a stone.

'Are you going to take her part?' Diane asked, her voice breaking as she looked at him with horror. 'She's known all along that I was your sister. Can't you see, Kane? It's like a sick replay—she's setting us against each other, just as she did with Hugh and me. Because if you marry her, you'll lose me! I'll never set foot on Glenalbyn again!'

He didn't look at Emma. He said quietly, 'She was a child.'

'She was sixteen! She deliberately, cleverly, cold-bloodedly set out to smash up our engagement. Oh, she knew that Hugh wouldn't have taken any notice of tantrums or bad behaviour, so she was always charming to me, but she pretended to develop bulimia.' Diane gave a harsh laugh. 'Very cunning, because of course they made her go to a therapist, and he told Hugh that it was too soon after her mother's death for us to marry. I'd have waited—I wanted to wait—but he said no, he owed Emma that—she hadn't had much of a life so far. He said he'd contact me when she left home, but he didn't.'

Emma said stonily, 'He died just over a year after you left.'

'Why didn't you let me know?' Appealing to Kane, a hint of wild triumph in her voice, she cried, 'All along she knew exactly what she was doing. She's always been a conniving little—'

'He dropped dead in the street from a heart attack.' Emma drew in a ragged breath. 'I didn't know he'd made any promises to you.'

It was obvious that Diane was holding herself together by will-power alone. White-faced, she turned blindly to her brother.

Even then, Emma noticed how both his mother and his sister sought Kane's strength; he put his arm around Diane and held her close as she began to cry, intense, heart-shaking sobs that echoed around the quiet room with the finality and heartbreak of years. Kane looked at Emma with a face carved from granite, and eyes that were flat and cold and deadly.

'Did you know that Diane was my sister?' he asked.

Unable to speak, reading his decision in the icy depths of his eyes, Emma nodded.

'You'd better go,' he said.

Her heart broke. How often had she read that and taken it for the cliché it was? Yet she felt it, a sudden sundering of something rare and precious, the icy rush of despair.

As Emma went through the doorway that dreadful sobbing battered her heart. Steadily she walked out of the homestead and into the bright spring sunlight and the fresh, brisk breeze—blanket-drying weather, her mother had used to call the spring and autumn equinoxes—sweet with the scents of mown grass and flowers.

Oh, God, how clearly her sins had come home to roost. She could never wipe out that single, inexcusable act. Diane was still locked into its effects, still grieving for the man she had lost.

Resentment battled with grief. It wasn't fair, she thought mutinously as she got into the car. Surely Diane could see that a girl who'd just lost her mother—the mother whose last years had been made miserable by Diane—couldn't be held entirely responsible for her actions?

Kane understood—but when it came to the crunch he supported his half-sister.

Emma drove back beneath the magnolias, crushing fallen petals into the metal on the drive. Above, tiny almond-green leaves uncurled with all the promise of a new season, the fresh, bright green so vivid that it robbed the remaining blossoms of colour and impact and drained the life from them.

Just when she made the decision to leave Parahai she

never really knew, but it was set in concrete by the time she turned into the gateway.

And the telephone call from Mrs Firth reinforced that decision. Without emotion, Emma told her that she was thinking of spending the three days before she could move into her house at Hamilton at a friend's bach on the Coromandel Peninsula.

'What a good idea! It means I can get the house packed up sooner. Take the car,' Mrs Firth said. 'Until I work out what I want done with it you might as well use it. And don't fret about anything; now that I've made up my mind, it's just a matter of contacting my solicitor and she'll deal with everything.'

'Tell Kane Talbot you're selling,' Emma said, surprised that she could say his name without shivering, with nothing but a leaden numbness. 'He said something about buying the house from you.'

'Did he? Oh, it would make everything much simpler if he does want it. I'll do that.'

'How's Pippa?'

A little sigh. 'Still not very well, poor darling, but she has cheered up since I've been here. Ring me when you arrive at the bach, Emma, and tell me how the dogs stood the journey.'

After a moment's hesitation Emma said, 'Mrs Firth, had you thought of leaving Lucky here? If you have, I'd like to take him. We get on very well—'

'Oh, Emma, would you? I've been so worried—my son-in-law really doesn't like dogs, and I wondered—but are you sure you want him? He's such a big dog and he costs a lot to feed—'

Smiling, Emma broke in, 'I know, I know, but he's a great companion, and I'd love to have him permanently.'

'Oh, you don't know what a weight off my mind that is! I was so worried about quarantine, and—well, everything.'

At least something had been salvaged from these last

weeks, Emma decided as she replaced the receiver. Lucky's future was assured.

Three hours after she'd left Diane Heathcote weeping in her brother's arms, Emma locked the door behind her and got into the Volvo. Keeping her gaze steadfastly averted from the drive into Glenalbyn, she drove down the road to Parahai, where she dropped the house key off at the land agent's before setting her face south. As she drove past the turn-off to Glenalbyn she thanked the good fortune that had prevented her from ever giving Kane her future address in Hamilton.

Both she and the dogs managed the trip very well, although Babe had to be monitored carefully. With the frequent stops this entailed, it took Emma all day to get to the bach, and when she arrived she looked around at the white sand, and the limitless grey-blue ocean, and thought bleakly that she might just as well have stayed in Parahai.

There was no peace, no forgiveness here—no refuge from the torment that ate into her composure and sent her thoughts running around grooves in her brain, over and over, taking the same track through her emotions and getting nowhere.

She unpacked and fed the dogs, then rang Mrs Firth, but all she got was an answering machine. Stammering slightly, because it was unexpected, she simply said that she'd arrived and that the dogs were well.

Emma spent the next few days walking with the dogs along the beach and trying to get enough rest to make up for the long, empty nights. The dogs accepted their new quarters with interest and no noticeable upset. Babe ventured out very rarely, content to spend most of her time snoozing in a patch of sunlight. She'd become more fragile and slower-moving even in the short time since Emma had arrived at Parahai; stroking the small, neat head with its pointed, grey muzzle and sharp ears, Emma told herself that fourteen years was a good age for a corgi, and for all of those years Babe had been loved and looked after.

The little dog should have spent her last months with the woman who'd done that loving, but life had a habit of getting in the way of fairness.

It had certainly smacked Emma fair and square in the face.

During the day she managed well enough; she could keep her mind on what she was doing and resolutely refuse to remember that last confrontation at the homestead. But at night her mind refused to obey her will. Lying curled in her bed, wrenched by a grief that ached outwards from her bones, she found it impossible to block the memories. Vivid, compelling, they followed each other in rich procession—the sound of Kane's voice, the splintering amber of his eyes, the curve of his mouth…

His tender ferocity and her ardent response…

Don't forget, Emma reminded herself tearlessly, the way he stood by his sister.

Of course he'd never told her that he loved her, never suggested a shared future. They had come together in a fury of desire and hunger, and for the moment that had been enough.

But it wasn't enough now, certainly not enough to base her life on. 'I am not,' she said fiercely into her pillow, 'going to be like his sister—spend the rest of my life yearning for a man I can't have. *I will not do it.*'

Following her mental map, Emma drove the Volvo carefully through the flat, suburban streets of Hamilton. She was not relishing the next couple of days, but at least she'd be busy unpacking her furniture, such as it was, and setting up the little unit.

It would, she thought grimly, keep her busy until she left for work on Monday.

'Here we are,' she said to the dogs. The Volvo drew in behind a parked car and she got out, relieved to see that the van that was to bring her stuff hadn't yet arrived. She hoped that the people who had moved out of the unit had left it clean.

Opening the car door, she got out and stretched and let the dogs out of the rear. Lucky jumped down, sniffed, and began to bark as he raced towards the car in front.

'Lucky! Come back here!'

Slowly, and with obvious reluctance, he stopped both his barking and the headlong rush. Stern-voiced, Emma repeated her command. After a last interested glance, he turned and began to lope towards her, ears and tongue lolling, his good-humoured grin very much in evidence.

'Good boy,' she said, rubbing around his ears. 'You'll have to get used to people in cars. I know and you know you're a marshmallow at heart, but you can look scary.'

He pressed against her, then startled her by pulling away and barking again, setting himself in front of her with blunt determination.

Emma looked up and her heart twisted. This had happened several times since she'd left Parahai—she'd catch a glimpse of a black head and wide shoulders, and such desolation would pour through her that she'd have to turn abruptly and go away, anywhere, just to avoid a man who bore a superficial resemblance to Kane.

Only this one wasn't superficial. The man who was getting out of the driver's seat of the car in front was the real thing. The brittle composure Emma had pasted over her emotions shattered like a crystal struck against steel.

Pain lanced through her, keen as the blade of an assassin, rendered even more cruel by the false promise of a thin thread of hope. Stonily, holding her face under such control that it ached, she asked, 'What are you doing here?'

'Checking up on you.' A tawny aura danced around Kane's head.

They faced each other like enemies, the dog between them, his hackles slightly lifted as he stared at the man.

Dominant males, Emma thought. 'I'm fine,' she said, the lying words acrid on her tongue.

Babe came up and sniffed around Kane's ankles before trotting back to sit beside Emma.

Kane hadn't looked tense, but her statement relaxed some subtle inner tautness. With a flick of freezing scorn in her voice, she finished, 'So you can go back home now.'

Although he didn't move, a low growl rumbled through Lucky.

'Sit,' Emma commanded steadily, and Lucky subsided, but he kept his eyes on the man in front of them.

'We have things to discuss,' Kane said abruptly.

'No.'

'Emma, I need to talk to you.'

If he'd said I *want* to talk to you she'd have turned and walked away, but there was something in his deep, detached voice, some hidden note that made her hesitate. Besides, she thought, looking for a fleeting moment at the hard warrior's features, he wouldn't give up.

The early afternoon sun was sauntering slowly overhead, promising a perfect spring afternoon. Emma said gruffly, 'All right, then. What do you want to say?'

'Not here,' he said, as a group of high school girls wandered past, looking at him with sideways, interested glances and several giggled remarks. Ignoring them, he watched her with vivid, unrelenting eyes. 'Let's go inside.'

'There's no furniture.'

He frowned. 'When is it coming?'

The numerals on her watch wavered, then steadied. 'Any moment.'

'Then let's wait in there.'

She'd already picked up the key from the agent, so she walked along the drive and up the narrow concrete path to the front door.

Although Emma kept her eyes firmly fixed in front of her, she felt Kane behind her, a presence that overpowered her. Something inside her twisted and tore. What was she doing?

The inevitable, she thought, trying to calm down. Kane had something to say, and he wasn't going until he'd said it. She could keep herself under control long enough for that.

And then he'd leave and she'd be able to luxuriate in the barren peace she'd managed to achieve during these past few days.

But how had he found her? Mrs Firth didn't know her new address, so Kane certainly couldn't have got it from her. And there was no one else he could contact.

She unlocked the door and pushed it open, drawing in a breath of stale, hot air; the sun streamed through uncurtained sliding doors and across the worn carpet on the floor. Walking swiftly through its heavy stuffiness, she pushed the windows open.

She clutched the remnants of her poise around her, terrified of splintering like a Christmas tree bauble thrown onto the floor; she desperately wanted to get through this with dignity.

'Would you like a drink?' she asked when the windows were open and she had to turn to look at him. 'Tea? Coffee? I've got a box of stuff in the car, and a picnic hamper.'

'Something cold,' he said. 'Water will be fine.'

Even the water was warm. Nevertheless, after he'd brought her picnic hamper in, and she'd taken the glasses from it, she gave him water and poured some for herself as well; it gave her hands something to do. And then, clear plastic glasses in hand, they faced each other in the small, hot, slightly shabby sitting room.

Lucky had to be ordered to heel again. When he was settled Emma took a couple of sips and asked, 'What did you want to see me about?'

Kane frowned. 'A variety of things. Rory first of all.'

Emma's hand went out to rest lightly on Lucky's head.

Frowning, Kane observed the betraying little movement,

but he went on, 'Lucky's quite safe. Rory's borrowed money to pay back his debt.'

'From you?'

He showed his teeth. 'No. From a bank. He's had to sell his car and his boat and several of his other prized possessions, and he's accepted that he has a gambling problem. He's working with an organisation to overcome that.'

It sounded very easy, very cut and dried. Emma asked, 'How did you terrify him into all that?'

Kane gave her a smile that sent alarm shivering through her system. 'Terrify is probably the operative word,' he said lazily, 'but he knew he was out of his depth, and he was pathetically grateful to have someone rescue him—even if the conditions were unpalatable and included telling the police all he knew about the dog fighting ring.' His voice smoothed, became positively lulling. 'I pointed out that I don't appreciate having my home used as a base to plan criminal operations—especially ones involving people I know.'

Rory had clearly had a most unpleasant time with Kane.

'Good,' Emma said fiercely. 'Do you think he'll stick to the programme?'

'I don't know, and I don't care much, but he certainly won't bother you or me again. Actually, I think he probably will stick to it. He was scared.'

Silence fell, prickling with tension. Emma drank some more water, pretending to be watching for the van through the window because that kept her eyes resolutely away from the man who stood opposite her.

Eventually he said coolly, 'Diane is all right.'

Over the rawness in her throat, Emma muttered, 'I'm sorry—I should have told you that she—that I—'

'Yes, you should have, but I can see why you didn't. For the same reason, I imagine, that I didn't tell you I was engaged to Jennifer. Because it would have meant making decisions we weren't prepared to face.'

CHAPTER TEN

KANE got to his feet and walked across to the window, stopping to look at the quiet suburban street outside.

It was a far cry from Taupo, where the vast lake had filled Emma's vision from almost every window. On fine days she'd been able to see the distant peaks of the volcanoes that gave the area its name—the Volcanic Plateau—beautiful yet marked by the violence of nature at its most terrifying. Even the lake was the result of the biggest volcanic explosion in the last two thousand years, one so enormous that Roman and Chinese astronomers had written of its effect on northern hemisphere weather and skies.

Here she saw trees and other houses, the street, gardens. Hamilton was neat and prosperous and she'd thought it a refuge, a safe haven. But Kane had found her anyway, and some wildness in her soul longed for the view from her house in Taupo.

Emma said, 'Even before my father died I was beginning to realise what I'd done to Diane and to him. He never knew that I'd faked bulimia, and I never had the chance to tell him and ask him to forgive me. I don't know whether he would have.' After a moment's hesitation she added, 'I didn't find her name in his address book. If I had, I'd have written to tell her that he was dead.'

It was really important that Kane understand this, and she exhaled sharply when he said quietly, 'I believe you.' Silhouetted like some dark threat against the light beyond the window, he went on, 'My mother sent for Diane.'

He turned so that she could see the strong angles of his profile. She would never get over him, she thought wearily. Never.

Choosing his words precisely, he went on, 'My mother is possessive. There are reasons—when she left my father she took me, but he won custody.' Unusually for him, he paused. In a voice so icily detached it chilled her blood, he resumed, 'I've never known the terms of the agreement they came to, but I believe he threatened to reveal not only that she'd had an affair, but that she'd set the homestead on fire before running away to Australia with me.'

Ignoring Emma's gasp, he continued, 'Oh, she didn't intend to burn the house down—when she decided to leave him she stuffed their wedding photographs and her wedding dress into the wood range and set them alight, then drove away with me. My mother had sent the housekeeper home, but she came back when she saw the smoke. There must have been some fault in the range, because by then the house was well on fire.'

Emma licked dry lips. 'Where was your father?' she asked inanely.

'At a conference in Wellington.' Clearly hating this, he paused, but went on, 'They should never have married. He was a stern man, with an almost pathological inability to reveal his feelings. My mother was twelve years younger—spoiled and laughing and frivolous. She thought he would soften after they married. She thought she could change him. Of course he didn't and she didn't, and she ended up so scarred by the whole experience that she never married again, had no other children, and became too focused on me.'

Kane never referred to Mrs Talbot as Mum, or Mother, or any of those other words. It was always 'my mother'.

Emma said quietly, 'She can't be too possessive if she was happy for you to marry Jennifer.'

'Jennifer is the daughter of an old friend of hers.' Kane's voice was level and impersonal, as though he were discussing some point of business. 'Socially, materially, in ways that are important to my mother, it would have been a good marriage. But she knew that although I liked

Jennifer I was not in love with her. And Jennifer wasn't in love with me, either. We both wanted a marriage based on affection and shared interests.'

Emma's brows shot up. 'A marriage of convenience?' she asked sarcastically.

'Exactly.'

'It sounds very cold-blooded,' she said.

'At the time it seemed sensible and worthwhile.' His mouth hardened and he went on, 'It would have lasted. I have strong views on the sanctity of marriage.' His voice was ironic. 'Children from bitter divorces tend to.'

Trying to keep her voice steady, Emma asked, 'Is that what your mother wants for you? A bloodless marriage with a *suitable* woman?'

'She thinks that love is dangerous, and certainly no basis for marriage,' he said. 'She fell in love and it damned near killed her. She lost everything—Diane, whom she loved dearly, her self-esteem, and finally, me. Her dreams of marriage to the man she loved turned to a nightmare.'

His even, emotionless words struck like bullets. Emma understood now why he'd suggested they get to know each other before they made love; with a background like that he'd probably always be suspicious of emotions.

Which made his opening up now so precious, so important.

'And she thought the same thing was happening to you?'

'Yes. Jennifer enjoys life in the country. She's serene and placid and good-humoured.' His voice altered. 'My mother knew the minute she saw you with me that I wanted you. She convinced herself I'd done exactly what she did when she met my father—fallen headlong into lust for someone totally unsuitable.'

'With the added disadvantage that I'm not rich and socially well-connected,' Emma said with a snap.

Kane's eyes narrowed. 'That's not an issue. She invited you up to dinner to see what you were like, and that evening confirmed all her worst fears. I couldn't keep my eyes off you, whereas you were composed and self-assured—you gave nothing away. So she decided to put an end to it if she possibly could. And you showed her the means to do that.'

'She was with me when I saw the photographs of Diane in the powder room.'

'Add that to the fact that yours isn't a common name, and that as well as living all your life in Taupo you were the right age. Also, I'd told her that your mother died when you were almost sixteen. Diane went to stay with her after your father turned her away, so my mother knew all about it—except,' he added grimly, 'that she'd been his lover while your mother was ill.'

Emma said quietly, 'I don't blame her now.'

'You're forgiving,' he said curtly. 'My mother probably wouldn't have done anything with her knowledge, but when I broke the engagement she was convinced I needed rescuing from the sort of fatal attraction she'd felt with my father.'

Emma straightened her shoulders. 'I see.'

'Yes.' His mouth thinned. 'She got Diane to come back. Which was the best thing she could have done, although I didn't think so at the time. Finally seeing you, realising that she'd demonised you all these years, was an exorcism for Diane. But I'm finding it very hard to forgive my mother for her part in it.'

Emma drew in a ragged breath, steadying her voice to say, 'She did what she thought was best for you.'

'She knows now that I'm the best judge of that.'

About time she learned it, Emma thought uncharitably, although she felt sorry for Mrs Talbot, so affected by the tragedy of her marriage that she'd done her best to make sure Kane didn't suffer a similar fate.

Aloud, she said, 'Diane has every right to be angry with me—because I quite deliberately broke her and my father up—but I wish she could see it from my point of view. To me their affair was the ultimate betrayal of my mother. As

I grew up I realised that she'd been sick for so long that my father must have felt more pity for her than love. At sixteen I didn't understand that—I just knew Diane was taking my mother's place, had taken it even before Mum died.'

'So you put an end to it.' His voice was cool; she looked across and saw that he'd retreated behind his seamless armour of self-sufficiency.

It was vital that he understand, even if Diane and his mother couldn't. Emma said, 'A girl at school had bulimia; there was a lot of fuss—doctors and counsellors, the whole family had to go—and my best friend said, "They're all falling over themselves to be nice to her. Why not try that?" So I pretended to have it too, and I made it quite clear that it had only started after Diane came on the scene. She knew what I was doing, but my father wouldn't believe her.'

He didn't speak, and when she stole a look she saw nothing but a stony coldness in his face. Then he said, 'You were still grieving for your mother.'

She said, 'I knew what I was doing.'

'You were fighting for some sort of security,' he said evenly. 'I understand that.'

'I might have been fighting for security, but part of it was simply for revenge. You see, although she never said anything to my father, my mother talked to me about his—about him and Diane. It broke her heart. But two wrongs don't make a right—breaking someone else's heart didn't help my mother at all.'

'Emma,' he said quietly, 'I do understand.'

Emma wanted to believe him, but this was too important for her to accept his reply without making sure he'd thought it through. 'You didn't understand it that morning.'

He drank the rest of the water down and set the empty glass on the windowsill. 'When I woke that morning I felt as though at last I held the world in my hands. Then I arrived home to be confronted with a hysterical Diane and a mother who insisted you'd known all along that she was my sister.'

Emma flinched. 'Yes.'

'All I could think of was that you could have told me. That if you'd trusted me you would have told me.'

'You didn't tell me about Jennifer,' she retorted spiritedly.

'I know, and at first it was cowardice. Then, when I realised that I was in too deep, I didn't want to talk to you about her—it seemed a kind of betrayal. I wanted to break it off with her first. I felt I should go to Australia and tell her.' He showed his teeth in a mirthless smile. 'It seemed the honourable thing to do.'

And he would hate, she thought perceptively, not living up to his own standards of honour. 'At first I didn't think that Diane being your half-sister would matter,' she admitted. 'I wasn't going to be at Parahai for long, and I didn't think that anything would come of—well, anyway, when you asked me if we could be friends, I knew I'd left it too late.'

And she still hadn't thought there was any sort of future for them beyond a transient affair.

Stealing a look at him, she wondered just why he'd come. The hard-honed features revealed nothing.

She took a deep breath. 'I didn't know what to do, but when you—when I realised you wanted an affair, I thought, At least I can have this. I was a coward too.'

'No,' he said, not smiling, but not angry either. 'I wish you'd told me, because Diane's arrival and recriminations threw me completely. I'd woken that morning aware that something fundamental had changed in me, and hoping like hell that you'd made love because you wanted me, not because Rory had thrown you off balance—'

She said, 'Oh, Kane!'

'It seemed possible,' he said. 'Danger is the greatest aphrodisiac.'

'Except that there wasn't any danger.'

'Shock, disillusion, anger—whatever.' He looked at her with something like grim amusement. 'I wasn't thinking very well that morning. Then I went home and there was Diane, jet lagged and strung-up and so angry she couldn't speak, and my mother, terrified but still convinced she'd done the right thing to haul Diane all the way back from London to confront me with the truth.' He took fierce, impatient steps across the room and swung around, dark face accusing. 'And you admitted it all, and then you ran away.'

'I didn't run! You told me to go!'

Lucky growled softly, ears flattening against his head. Emma bent to soothe him, but he still watched Kane. Babe had found herself a patch of sunlight, but she wasn't asleep; she was lying with her head on her paws, dark eyes fixed on Kane's face.

He'd reined in his temper. 'I didn't mean you to go away from Parahai, and you know it. I had to get Diane settled down and deal with my mother first, and then I had to face the fact that if I insisted on marrying you I could tear my family apart. And I knew that although I'd give my life for you, you didn't feel anything like that for me.'

His voice revealed no emotion, but Emma didn't make the mistake of thinking that he felt none.

Shaken, realising for the first time the torment he'd endured, she said, 'You didn't say *anything* about being in love with me! Even after you'd broken off with Jennifer you only suggested we be friends. I knew you wanted me, and I was terrified you'd find out that I was the rotten kid who'd ruined your sister's life, and I just didn't know what to do or how to deal with it. But you never said you loved me.'

Kane looked down at Lucky, who was watching him with alert brown eyes. He smiled, a sardonic travesty without humour, without warmth. 'I was afraid.'

She went pale. 'Why? You must have known how I felt,' she whispered.

'All I knew was that I could seduce you,' he said.

Emma gave him a haughty stare. 'Really?' she asked with dangerous quietness.

His smile was mocking and tender, a mixture that finally set her hope alight. 'Emma, that was pretty obvious. But it wasn't enough.' His eyes glittered beneath the heavy lids. 'Jennifer said that I'd fallen for youth and a pretty face, someone who hero-worshipped me just the way my mother had adored my father. She could have been right. I wanted a lot more than that from you, which is why I suggested we try being friends for a while. I thought you should have that time with no pressure from me.'

Emma decided that she was not going to like Jennifer. Brusquely she said, 'It was very noble of you. When I flung myself into your arms and practically begged you to make love to me you must have thought me very young and stupid.'

'No! I thought that I should have the will-power not to take you, but I couldn't stop.' If her voice had been tinged with self-derision, his crackled with it. 'And I didn't care; all I could think of was that I'd never known what passion was until I kissed you and you burned like lightning in my arms. And when we made love—it meant so little to you that you left me the next day, whereas I'd have gone down into hell for you, Emma.'

'You threw me out.' She took several steps forward, pushing Lucky aside when he tried to keep between them. 'You know you did. You looked at me and told me to go.'

He said harshly, 'Not out of my life, not out of my heart! I wanted you to leave us then because I had to deal with Diane. You're strong, you've been tempered in fire, you have guts and determination and courage. Diane lost her mother to death, then her stepmother abandoned her, leaving her with an embittered, silent father who packed her off to boarding school. She married some young idiot when she was eighteen because she wanted someone to love her, and within two years he'd told her he was gay; the marriage was a sham. I couldn't just dump her. But I was coming down as soon as I could to tell you that whatever happened, I loved you.'

'Why didn't you?'

'Diane,' he said simply. 'She collapsed and we had to hospitalise her. No, it's all right—it was nervous exhaustion and jet lag and dehydration, combined with the fact that she's a very jittery flier. And then I had to deal with my mother, who was awash with guilt and horror at what she'd done. And then, when I came down to see you in the middle of the afternoon, you'd gone.'

Emma said unevenly, 'One of the reasons I left was that I didn't really believe that you could love me. I'd tried so hard to convince myself that I wasn't in love with you, that I was just one in a line of women who'd fallen for you, hoping they'd be the one to break through that warrior's armour of self-sufficiency.'

He looked at her with naked intensity. 'And is that it?'

Shivering, she said, 'No. Leaving you taught me that. Whatever had happened to me wasn't the easy desire of the eyes. I've been changed from the soul outwards.'

'Yes,' he said. 'In the end the decision was simple, although it hurt. I looked at a life without you and decided I couldn't bear it, that you'd be worth losing my family for.'

'I couldn't bear it if you did.'

He shook his head. 'It will take them a while to get used to you, but they'll come around. Even if they don't, Diane lives in London and my mother spends most of the year in Australia, so they won't cause you any worry.'

She would make overtures, Emma thought, beginning at last to believe. Kane wouldn't lose his family because of her—she wouldn't let it happen.

She asked, 'Do you still think I'm too young for you?'

'Yes,' he said curtly. 'Not that it's going to make any difference; I gave up being self-sacrificing the moment I realised you'd left Parahai. And I didn't say you were too young—I said I was too old. There's a subtle difference.'

'Semantics,' she said, able to smile now.

They still hadn't touched. It would have been so easy to walk across the room, to lose herself in simple desire, to forget everything but the incandescent heat of passion.

Easy, but wrong. They needed this process of exploration, this discovery of each other's innermost thoughts. Passion, she thought, infused with an inner wisdom handed down through countless female ancestors, would be a big and vital part of their marriage, but there were other, even more important aspects.

'Why did you leave?' he asked. 'Your first instinct is to come out fighting, not run away. I couldn't believe it when I realised you'd gone.'

Frowning, Emma tried to recall the lassitude, the bleak anguish that had driven her away. 'It seems ridiculous, over-dramatic now. At the time I didn't think I was overwrought, but I must have been in a state of shock. I thought it was over. And I couldn't bear it.'

'Emma,' he said, his voice deep and unsteady.

'No, listen. I convinced myself that it was payback time. I'd wrecked Diane's hopes; I deserved to lose the only man I've ever loved. And you were so angry—'

'I do get angry,' he said. 'Most of the time I can control my temper, but for some reason you seem to be able to tip me over the edge.' His smile was savage and sardonic. 'Because I didn't know where I was with you. Arrogance—'

'You aren't arrogant,' she broke in, adding honestly, 'Well, not all the time. And it's not really arrogance—it's more determination and a kind of imperious—'

Kane's quiet laughter effectively silenced her. She looked at him, saw the fire kindle in his eyes, and the tender curve of that straight, sensuous mouth. 'Arrogant is a synonym for overbearing, and I know I can be that. I try to overcome it, but it's there.'

She laughed too. 'I've always thought of it as the dominant male syndrome,' she said demurely, adding, 'It's something you share with Lucky.'

Something must have conveyed to Lucky that his duty as guard was over. He wandered across to sit beside Babe and watched them benignly, with none of the alert seriousness of a few minutes before.

'Emma,' Kane said, and took a step towards her. 'When you walked out of that room, with your back straight and your head high and your chin up, I stayed because I was furious with you for keeping quiet about your connection with Diane.' He hesitated, then finished, 'The truth is that I punished you by not contacting you until the afternoon. Which gave you the time to go, and so punished me infinitely more.'

Emma shivered. 'I didn't know how you felt about me. I knew you wanted me, but wanting isn't love. In a way leaving seemed fair, sort of an eye for an eye—a lover for a lover.' Her confidence of a few moments before ebbed swiftly. She turned away from him and stared through the window. 'I'll try very hard to—to make things right, but what if I can't? Your mother doesn't like me—how could she?—and Diane will always see me as the spoilt little bitch who ruined her life.'

He said quietly, 'My mother will learn to like you.'

'It's not going to be that easy. Diane—'

'Will have to find her own way,' he interrupted, coming across the room and pulling her into his arms. They closed around her tightly. Into her hair he said, 'I love my sister and I'm certain she accepts now that what happened seven years ago is finished, that you're no longer a terrified kid using all the weapons you could find to cling to your father. If she doesn't—if I never hear from her again or see her again—I'll be more sorry than I can say, but it will be worth it, because my life without you is bleak and dreary beyond bearing. Emma, I love you. Please don't turn me away.'

The raw urgency of his words banished all her fears. All her life, she thought tremulously as she lifted her head and smiled, she would give Kane what he wanted, because he was hers.

Lucky's wild barking, followed by an urgent hammering on the door and the shout, 'Hey, where do you want this furniture to go?' broke them apart. Looking at each other, they began to laugh.

The western sky flamed into radiance, then dimmed as the tenderness of evening swept across it.

Eventually Emma lifted her head from Kane's chest and asked hoarsely, 'When did you first know that you loved me?'

His mouth traced the curve of her chin, the sweep of one cheekbone. 'It is,' he said deeply, 'so long since I've been able to look at you and see anything but the woman I love that I can't remember how I felt. But the first time I saw you I felt as though someone had kicked me in the gut.'

'Me too,' she admitted, her voice reminiscent. 'You had the sun behind you and you looked like something tough and troublesome from some heroic saga, and I thought, Oh, hell, this is something I've never been faced with before.'

'Good,' he said with cool satisfaction.

'But you knew that. You knew you could seduce me.'

'Does that rankle?' He laughed quietly and kissed the tip of her ear. 'Lust is a physical response. I suspected I was losing my heart when we went riding through the bush—which has cost me vast amounts of money to keep tightly fenced so that dogs can't get in and kill the kiwi population—with Lucky trotting free. I hadn't even thought about him because I was too busy wondering how your delicate skin would feel under my mouth, and whether you'd enjoy living in a small town like Parahai.'

'I'll like living with you,' she said simply, adding, 'Although I'm not accustomed to entertaining visiting Prime Ministers and minor royalty.'

He said, 'What on earth are you talking about?'

'Annabelle said that Jennifer is accustomed to that sort of social life.'

Kane frowned. 'It happens, but you'll manage. As for Annabelle—she's a damned nuisance, but you've seen her at her worst. She's a good kid most of the time.'

Emma nodded. 'I feel really sorry for her because although it's only a crush she's miserable.'

'You must think I come from a totally dysfunctional family,' he said drily. 'Apart from Annabelle and Rory's parents, who are too rich and too selfish, you've met all the difficult ones. The rest of us are quite normal.'

'Good,' she said. 'And, yes, I'll learn how to deal with the people you entertain.'

'I know you will.' He was going to say more, but from the open doorway came an interrogatory bark that startled them both into laughter.

'I'd better go and feed them,' Emma said, sitting up to meet Babe's reproachful brown eyes. 'Before I went to Parahai I had a nice, trouble-free life—no dogs to nanny, no man to confuse me, everything going along as smoothly as whipped cream. Now I'm not just a nanny, I own them both, and my life and my heart and my soul have been taken away from me.'

'Not taken away,' Kane said, kissing her with slow, deliberate enjoyment, determined to exact a response. 'Never taken away, my darling, my heart's delight, just joined to mine.'

'When do you have to go?' she whispered, lifting her hand to cup the autocratic line of his jaw, thrilling to the silken rasp of his beard beneath the fine texture of his skin.

'I'm staying here as long as it takes,' he said. 'I'm on my way back from Ayer's Rock, so I should get home to Glenalbyn as soon as I can, but I'm not leaving here until there's an engagement ring on your finger and we've made plans.'

'Ayer's Rock?' she murmured. 'What were you doing in Australia?'

'Pleading with your friend Sorrel to give me your new address,' he said, without a trace of shame.

Emma sat bolt-upright and looked down into a dark, amused face. 'Sorrel? How on earth did you catch up with her?' she demanded.

He laughed, deep and low and triumphant. 'Not easily, but there are ways. As soon as I realised that Mrs Firth had no idea of your new address, beyond that it was Hamilton, I remembered your friend the model. I managed to track her down through her agency in New York, and rang her in Singapore. She wouldn't tell me anything until she'd met me. And as she was going to Ayer's Rock the next day I flew there.'

'She's beautiful, isn't she?'

'Very,' he said, watching her, 'and kind too. She made me tell her what had gone wrong, then she meditated for half an hour, and then she said she thought I would make you happy and gave me your address. She also told me that you'd be arriving today, so I came down and staked the place out.'

His eyes told her he'd enjoyed Sorrel's spectacular beauty without wanting her at all. Emma's last shred of reservation, the small, secret fear that he might one day wake up and wonder what he was doing married to her, withered and shrank into nothingness.

She sighed and said, 'I'm glad you liked her.'

'I like her,' he said deliberately, and then his eyes kindled and he touched a lean finger to the soft bottom curve of her mouth. 'You,' he said in a voice that was at once gentle and reverberating, raw with need and smooth with sexuality, 'you, I love. More than my life itself. When are you coming north to marry me?'

'I'll have to give in my notice.'

'A fortnight?'

'It should probably be a month. They're going to think I'm mad! I haven't even started work there yet!'

His eyes glinted at her, lazy passion swirling hypnotically in the golden topaz depths. 'But you'll make it as soon as possible.'

'Yes,' she said.

'Good,' he said urgently, turning her into his arms to kiss her again. However, sooner than she wanted, he said, 'Will you miss your work?'

She didn't try to lie. 'Yes.'

'Do you want to take a veterinary degree?'

Astonished, she gazed at him. 'When?'

'After we're married,' he said calmly.

Emma hesitated. To be a vet had been her greatest ambition, one she'd renounced with many a hidden regret. She said quietly, 'A year ago I'd have said, Yes, thank you, so fast. But—'

'You don't have to decide this minute. I don't want you to have any regrets. Marriage shouldn't mean a narrowing of your life, it should be a festival, a union that enlarges both of us. If you feel frustrated and bored because you're stuck at home, I certainly won't be happy, and, although I'm not looking forward to having you away for much of the year while you do your degree, I'll manage.'

Her eyes filled with tears. 'Oh, I do love you,' she said, kissing him tenderly. 'But I don't want to spend all that time away from you, so I'll set up a stud instead.'

'Dogs?'

She grinned. 'Perhaps. Not immediately. I'll help you with your beasts and your sheep. I know you've got a good name already, but, believe me, in ten years' time Glenalbyn will be world-famous.'

He laughed and his arms contracted around her. 'I believe you,' he said.

From the doorway, Lucky yawned elaborately and noisily.

'Oh, poor things,' Emma cried, her eyes sparkling with laughter, 'they must be starving!'

Later, after the dogs had been fed and they'd eaten some sort of meal themselves, Emma asked from the depths of

Kane's arms, 'Have you heard anything more about the dog-fighting ring?'

Kane smiled as one of her curls wrapped itself around his finger. He tugged it gently, but the expression in his eyes made her shiver. 'I checked up with the police. They've arrested the three men who were running it, rescued a couple of dozen dogs and had to put down five who were too far gone to save.'

Sickened, she asked, 'Will Rory have to testify?'

'Apparently not. But the police let him know that they disapproved of him burgling houses and getting mixed up with thugs, so that's another reason for him to stay on the straight and narrow.'

'Good.' She thought of something else. 'Have they found the dogs who killed those sheep the night I left the back door open?'

He surveyed her with a slow, crooked smile. 'You've always been convinced Babe and Lucky weren't the culprits, haven't you? Well, you were right, so you won't have to worry about bringing Lucky back to Glenalbyn. They were a fox terrier bitch and an Alsatian cross. Freddie Hume shot them the night after you left. They belonged to a family that swore they were kept inside at night.'

'Poor dogs,' she said on a sigh. 'And poor people.'

His arms tightened around her. 'My compassionate Emma.'

In a muffled voice she asked, 'Are you buying Mrs Firth's house?'

'Yes. I need another house for the dairy unit.'

'Who'd have thought that agreeing to be nursemaid to two dogs would have led to this?' Emma said dreamily, tucking her head under Kane's chin and smiling as she watched the years come towards them, filled with rich promise. 'If Lucky hadn't chased your sheep we might never have met.'

Kane laughed and lifted her, kissed her with a determination and fire that turned her bones to liquid. 'Nonsense,' he said firmly. 'Of course we were meant to meet. We're soulmates.'

His smile dazzled her and excited her and reassured her as he carried her into her bedroom.

Lucky sighed and stretched out on his beanbag. He looked across at Babe, who gave him a foxy, sleepy grin. Well satisfied, both dogs drifted off to sleep.